Whispers

In

Waning

Whispers in Waning is a work of pure fiction. All names, characters, places, and incidents are the products of the author's imagination and used fictitiously. Any resemblance to actual localities, events, or people both living and dead is entirely coincidental.

Dedication

To my darling daughters (aka The Two Halves of My Heart), for giving me the magick of love and happiness. Moreover, for all those who still believe in the hidden power of all things.

Chapter One

Four in the morning and I still cannot seem to fall asleep, or rather, do I even want to? If I do, will those dreams, or as my Aunt Ellice likes to call them visions return? Damn I cannot afford to go another night without sleep, but I sure as hell do not want to experience another one of those awful dreams either. I guess I will do what I have done for the past three nights, perform yet another protection spell upon myself, make a cup of jasmine tea, and sit on the big bay windowsill.

The view outside my bay window is, to say the least, picturesque. The night seems to drape the sky in total darkness with the occasional twinkling of lights from passing airplanes, and the few stars occupying the sky. The smell of the nearby ocean permeated the area in a cool fresh scent. Spring was changing to summer and that meant the summer's Solstice was near.

This is a big deal in my family for you see I come from a long line of witches both male and female. The Craft does not discriminate to those who are willing to walk the path. I have seen photographs of ancestors long dead in my Aunt's albums, men and women, who were all practitioners of the Craft. I have even seen those who were a part of the famous Salem witch trials.

What a way to go burned alive at the stake. Personally, I would have preferred hanging as it is much quicker. By now, you are probably wondering just who in Goddess name am I? Well, far be it for me to be rude, so without further ado, allow me to introduce myself.

Formalities, you know I hate them, but if one is to show true maturity and intellect, not to mention good upbringing, then I guess they are necessary. For starters, my name is Anora Rhianlugh and I am the only daughter of the late Kernu and Diana Rhianlugh.

My parents, who were also active in the Craft, disappeared when I was about ten years old. It was then that the family decided the best place for me was here with my Aunt Ellice and Uncle Adler. My Uncle Adler was my father's eldest brother although not by much, a few months give or take.

The circumstances surrounding my parent's disappearance has never been resolved. The official report said that they were missing and presumed dead, but if you ask me, that is a load of shit. You see both my mother and father were in the best of health. In fact, Aunt Ellice constantly likes to inform me that I have been blessed with the gift of youth because of my parents. Eat your heart out Ponce de León. My Aunt also likes to consistently inform me of how "special" I am. You see I am the only child that my parents actually managed to have after three failed attempts all ending in miscarriages. I am also gifted with what my Uncle calls shinning tiger's eyes and hair the color of copper and gold, which is always soft to the touch, oh, one other feature that remains a mystery is the black mascara like lining around my eyes.

It has been there since I can remember and despite all attempts, it never seems to wash off or even fade for that matter. Both of my parents had dark brown hair and brown eyes, so how in the hell did I manage to turn out this way? I will be celebrating my thirty-third birthday this coming Hollow's Eve or Halloween as the rest of the rest of the free world prefers to call it. For as long as I can remember, I have never really had what most people would consider a "normal" upbringing. While the other little girls were playing with Barbie dolls, I was inside learning spells for everything from healing to protection. My Aunt's idea of shop class was not the making of wood or metal items but instead the making of potions. For me, school never let out.

The birds have begun chirping; it is well past five in the morning now. Damn time just flew by. It took the bullet train from one hour to the next without a hint of a layover. I will have to get ready for work in a few hours and yet another night has gone by with no rest for this Wiccan. God and Goddess help me, if I do not get a good night's sleep, I will be able to star in one of those zombie movies without the need of makeup.

The tea that I made earlier has since grown cold nevertheless; I can still use the caffeine rush. Maybe now that dawn has arrived, I can get at least a few hours of sleep before going to work. Despite all of my Wiccan education, I managed to find time to snag a bachelor's degree in graphic design. It allows me to be creative, my boss Bruce seems to like that but more so; it allows me a life outside of the Craft.

My boss once said that I must be using magick on potential clients in order to get their business and if so, to please keep it up. Well, I do not use magick for personal gain. I am neither crazy nor bold to be dabbling with the law of three like some people I know. Besides, I have enough strange things happening without adding that to the list.

Five-thirty in the morning, I really need to get some hint of rest otherwise, I will not be able to focus on work or magick today and I cannot afford to lose this job nor my sanity. I put the cup of cold tea on the nightstand and proceeded to lie down on the queen-sized bed. The sheets were of soft cotton and as white as fresh snow. Aunt Elise likes to use her own homemade version of fabric softener on her laundry and to tell you the truth, I do not know what ingredients she puts into it, but all of my clothes and linens smell like a fresh autumn breeze. She really should market that stuff but she said it is a family secret and it will remain that way.

As I lay down, I felt the sudden rush of air across my body. The sensation brought a soft moan from my throat. It was as if someone has just caressed me using the wind as their limb but there was no one in the room other than myself. Once more, I started to bury myself underneath the now warm sheets and placed my head upon the fluffy goose down pillows.

No sooner had I closed my eyes and taken that deep breath that you take when you're about to enjoy a good night's sleep, when suddenly the cold wind came again, this time, strong enough to fling the covers from the bed and rolling me onto my back. This time, it was not a pass-n-fancy but more like a steady flow of air throughout the room.

The wind somehow developed mass as it held me in place on my back completely immobilizing me. It then manifested a sharpness to it for with every wave of air that brushed across my body pieces of my nightshirt began to tear away exposing my bare skin.

I tried to move, tried to scream but all I could hear was the howling of the wind, which had now managed to render me completely deprived of clothing. As I begun to concentrate, attempting to cast yet another protection spell, I felt something stroke the tips of my breasts. A hand made of air was fondling me now. I could feel the impression of fingers but there was no visible hand to speak of. As if the dreams and brief visions were not bad enough, now here I lay, completely nude, and about to be raped by the wind itself.

I tried once more to move but it was no use. Whoever or whatever was in command of the air element also had control over my movements or lack thereof. All I could do was concentrate on the protection spell with the hopes that it would be enough to deter the one responsible for what was happening. I began to envision my aura glowing bright, enough to form a shield around my body before the wind could invade it.

The howling grew more intense and in the swirls of air, I felt hands and lips exploring my body. The hands fondled my breasts and traced the curves of my five-foot-four-inch frame while the lips touched my face and neck. I started chanting silently "Goddess of light, make me one too strong to fight." I felt the heat from my aura grow and my eyes began to shine with that same energy.

Aunt Elise and Uncle Adler once told me that whenever I would focus my energies, the whites of my eyes become as bright as a full moon and the darkness of my pupils would give the appearance of an endless black void with a bluish green ring around it. Allot of good it was doing now as the airy hands ran down my stomach and stopped right on the opening of my more sensitive region. The hands pressed down causing me to draw a quick breath, and then ever so slowly, they traced the circumference of my opening.

I continued chanting silently, envisioning my aura growing brighter until it covered my entire body hopefully pushing back the airy hands before they penetrated me. Granted I am a bit aroused, but this is not quite, what I had in mind. The wind made hands rose upwards from my body, then pressed downward again but this time, they were hitting the surface of my aura and not my bare flesh. Finally, I was winning this little tug-of-war but for how long?

The wind transformed into a small hurricane and was attempting to break through my aura to get to my sweet spot. I concentrated even harder now as I could feel the hands pressing against the surface of my aura. Then suddenly, out of nowhere I felt a thick substance plow through my aura and plunge into me.

The hands were just a decoy for what was now inside me. I let out a wild gasp at the girth, which occupied the space inside and inching slowly upwards in me. The sudden sensation caused me to lose concentration thus weakening my shield allowing the hands to return to their former positions atop of my breasts.

Lady and Lord give me strength. The wind had more than just a mind of its own, this airy but very hard and long girth started exiting and re-entering me. Every entry brought forth a deep moan from my lips. I had to stop this or at least try but my limbs were still weighed down by the force of the wind, and the hands now had control over my upper body. I was completely overpowered and unable to focus long enough to attempt another spell to save myself.

I threw my head from side to side, moaning and panting all the while as the wind formed manhood continued its invasion. I could feel myself growing wet from the sensation building within my body. The airy girth started exiting and entering faster and harder, each time pushing further up inside me. It grew, throbbing each time it entered me. The hands squeezing my breasts and intermittently pinching my nipples in the process. The force arched my entire body up and down the bed causing me to take deep breaths in-between.

Somehow, in the midst of the panting and moaning, I managed to let out a scream although I must admit it was partly in pleasure.

At that moment, Aunt Ellice and Uncle Adler rushed into the room holding what appeared to be talismans. They stood at the foot of the bed and began reciting what I later learned was a powerful protection chant designed to ward off any negative energies. No sooner had they raised the talismans in the air, the howling win dissipated and the feeling of airy hands and girth vanished. I was left lying on my bed, still on my back and naked with that icky feeling. I fought to gather my thoughts and place them into verbal words that my Aunt and Uncle could comprehend. Just then, Aunt Ellice leaned over and with just a glance, begun to will the sheets to rise up towards my head stopping just short of the base of my neck.

"You should rest a bit before going to work Anora." Her voice was soft and comforting, like the way a mother speaks to her child after they had a nightmare. I glanced over at my Uncle Adler who was moving up towards the right side of my bed, stopping just inches from the headboard. He bent down, leaned forward, and placed a gentle kiss on my forehead.

Uncle Adler was a tall man about six feet five inches tall and a good two hundred pounds of pure muscle. His hair was a silky salt and pepper mixture that he kept in a ponytail most of the time. Where most men his age would have started going bald, Uncle Adler retained all of his hair and then some. His eyes held pupils of light blue and his face was strong and firm like that of a chiseled sculpture. Despite the fact that he was fifty-six years old, Uncle Adler still had the body of a man who once underwent weight training. His arms and legs were like that of an athlete, his chest broad and tight. The only "flaw" to him was a hint of a stomach, which was most likely due to Aunt Ellice's cooking.

I closed my eyes briefly as he kissed my forehead. Feeling the warmth gave me a sense of security that everything was going to be all right now. When I opened my eyes to look at him, I noticed that Aunt Ellice had now taken residence beside him, her face full of a comforting and harmonious peace. There was no trace of the wind now, the room was still and back to its original state before all this occurred.

Aunt Ellice has to be about five feet four inches, except when she would, wear heals which would give her about an inch or two more. Like her male counterpart, Aunt Ellice also sported salt and pepper hair but much longer, just shy of her backside. Her eyes held two hazel irises and the fullness of her lips gave her the appearance of an Angelina Jolie look-a-like. She sported a small thinly shaped nose and high cheek bones which when she smiled radiated an emotion all their own.

If you were to look at the both of them standing together as I had been doing for the past twenty minutes now, you too would say to yourself that they look as though they were meant to be together. Aunt Ellice and Uncle Adler were the human representation of Yin and Yang if ever I saw one. They complimented one another in just about every aspect of their lives. Right now, they were my security blanket against whatever or whoever just tried to take me against my wishes. I stared up at my two guardians who were both sporting smiles now

"I guess your right Auntie perhaps I should try and rest a bit before work."

"Yes, I think you should." She said now placing her talisman into the pocket of her robe. She leaned down and laid another gentle kiss upon my forehead just as Uncle Adler had done mere moments before. See, told you they complimented one another in just about everything.

"Rest well my child." Whispered Uncle Adler.

"No more will you be bothered we'll see to that won't we darling?"

"That's right honey." Replied Aunt Ellice as she began making her way towards the door.

Uncle Adler soon followed her just passing her enough to open and hold the bedroom door for her as she glided out into the hall. Uncle Adler passed through the doorway still holding the doorknob. With one flowing movement, he entered the hallway simultaneously closing the door behind him. Once more, I closed my eyes and tried to get some rest but my brain was still flustered over the event and I could not calm it down enough to reach a restful state.

After all, I had just been sexually assaulted by the wind, or better still by someone who was using air magick. Question is, who and why?

Chapter Two

I awoke to the smell of Aunt Ellice's cinnamon and hazelnut muffins. After taking a moment to compose myself, I rose from the warmth of the bed and onto the cool wooden floor of my room. Thinking back on recent events, I could not help but have that feeling of was it all just a bad dream?

I stood staring outside at the fields hoping to receive some sort of sign that it was all in my head. As if, I had room in there for anything more. I walked over to the wooden table in the far corner of the room. Placed atop were two statues, one male, and one female. There were also candles, incense sticks, and two wooden bowls all neatly arranged along the surface of the table. Underneath laid a long cloth of pure white with the triple moon symbol in the middle. This was my altar for worship and communication with the deities. Sometimes I wish the Goddess and God had cellular phones for just these kinds of emergencies.

It was eight forty-five in the morning and I had to be in the office by ten. Good thing I live close to the downtown area and having a car helped too, so I had some time to focus on myself. It was Friday, so I had the next two days to figure this mess out but for now, I needed a shower very much.

The water was just warm enough so as not to burn my skin. I am a bit on the sensitive side you see so I cannot enjoy a hot shower like most people. As I begun to wash up, I could hear rustling in the bedroom followed almost immediately by Aunt Ellice's voice.

"Anora, breakfast is ready."
"I'll be right down."

There was a brief moment of silence between us, and then I could hear her chuckle as she exited the bedroom.

"Well you'd best get a move on, I don't know how long I can keep your Uncle from eating all the muffins."

"Tell him he'd better not."

Then the door to the room closed with a gentle bang and I knew she had gone. I finished my shower, dried off, put on my undies and robe, and descended the stairs. On my way to the kitchen, I began to fully take in the warm smell of Aunt Ellice's muffins. She had also prepared warm oatmeal and freshly squeezed orange juice. Uncle Adler had that look on his face, which suggested that he had reached his threshold of resistance and if I did not act quickly, I would lose the two remaining muffins Aunt Ellice had saved. I sat down and glanced at Uncle Adler with a slight grin of appreciation for his resistance. He met my stare and smiled back. Then out of nowhere, I heard him speak but there was no visible movement of his mouth.

"Your welcome sweetie but I should tell you that originally there were eight muffins." He smiled.

I found out that I could hear the thoughts of others when I was ten years old. It was on the very day that my parents disappeared. I heard them speak to me, and then my mother's screams filled my head causing me to scream. When Aunt Ellice came to me I had told her that my Mother and Father were gone and the last words they spoke were for me to be strong. Since then, Aunt Ellice has believed that I am special. She often refers to me as being a natural witch, a Wiccan whose abilities come from within.

I am not sure what it all means. Nevertheless, far be it for me to dampen one of the few things that make her happy. I picked up one of the muffins and took a bite. Aunt Ellice's muffins literally melt in your mouth as you chew. The sweet taste soothed my nerves and brought about happier thoughts to my mind. Aunt Ellice sat down next to Uncle Adler and the three of us exchanged glances. It was obvious that we were all thinking about the incident, which took place earlier this morning but were too afraid to bring it up. Finally, Uncle Adler broke the silence.

"Someone was using air magick and whoever it was clearly violated the Wiccan Rede." His voice clearly held anger in it.

"Agreed Uncle Adler." I said as I put down my glass and reached for the last remaining muffin.

"But I think the question here is not so much what type of magick was used but why?" "And why attack me?"

"We'll go speak with the council members and see what they think."

"In the meantime Anora, perhaps it would be wise to cast a triple protection spell, just to be sure." Said Aunt Ellice as she then rose from her chair with dishes in hand.

"I will, on my way to work Aunt Ellice." I said as I finished the last of the oatmeal and orange juice.

Uncle Adler had an unusual expression on his face as if he wanted to hold and prevent me from leaving. His face frozen to the point where I became compelled to try to read him, but it is a law within our coven not to read anyone's thoughts without their permission beforehand. So I did the next best thing, I asked him.

"Is there something you wish to say, Uncle?"

"I don't think it's wise that you leave Anora." He said still sporting that stare.

"I know Uncle, but I just can't put my life on hold like that."

"Yes I know, but I don't have to enjoy it."

Uncle Adler was the type of man that when he made his mind up about something, there was no swaying him. Moreover, he had clearly made up his mind not to approve of my venturing out into the world after what had happened.

"If it will make you feel better Uncle, I'll do the triple protection ritual before I go."

"I guess that will have to suffice now won't it?" He said changing his face back to that familiar grin which I remembered from earlier this morning. He was not happy about all this but he showed that he was willing to comply, at least for the moment.

I stood from the table, walked over to where he was sitting, and gave him a gentle kiss on the cheek. I then walked over to the sink and repeated the same gesture to Aunt Ellice. It was nearing ten o'clock and I had not even dressed for work. I ran upstairs to my bedroom and made a beeline for the walk-in closet.

Friday is casual dress day at my company so I did not have to pull out the business skirt and suit jacket combo. I took out a light blue blouse and a pair of navy blue dress pants.

"No need to show toes today." I thought to myself, so I took a pair of black casual shoes from the bottom and proceeded to dress for work.

Once dressed, I walked over to my alter and stood silently for a moment. I envisioned myself surrounded from head to toe by a bluish-white light. My body began to grow warm from the thought and once more could feel my eyes shine with energy. When I felt my energy was at its peak, I opened my eyes and raised my index finger to waist level. Turning clockwise, I envisioned the energy which I had accumulated pour from my finger to form a circle of radiant light around my body. Now with my circle of protection cast, I could perform the ritual of triple protection and get my Wiccan ass to work.

I started my chant to call upon the God and Goddess all the while concentrating on my aura's energy. I felt a coolness rush over me, then a warm sensation shortly thereafter. I successfully made contact with the Lady and Lord and could sense they were awaiting my request. I closed my eyes once more and envisioned myself standing in front of them on the astral plane. Now everyone has their own visions of the God and Goddess but I like the way in which they appear to me.

Lady Diana stood to my left, covered in a gown of glowing moonlight. Her long hair draped past the small of her back was luminescent in a golden yellow. Her eyes held two full moons in them and her skin glowed with that very same moonlight. Her full lips and sleek hourglass frame made her the epitome of true perfection.

Most models would sign away their very souls just to look half as beautiful. She is the Goddess of the moon and the mother of all Wiccans.

Standing to my right was Lord Pan himself. Although he possessed the feet and horns of a goat, he was still very easy on the eyes if I do say so myself. Pan is the God of the sun and father of all things both wild and Wiccan. His body was tight with muscles, his skin bore the glow of sunlight and his eyes held two bright burning orbs. There they both stood before me. It was like watching day and night at the same time and feeling the effects of both. I asked for their blessing for a good day and for their protection against that which would seek to do me harm. They began to radiate as one. The moon and the sun both at their peak of illumination standing before me.

I was blinded by the intensity of their light but comforted by its warmth and gentleness as it brushed my body, entering me through every pour until I could feel a piece of them inside me.

Both the Goddess and the God have touched me. There was a sort of calmness, an inner peace that was visible upon my face. I lowered my head to the Goddess and God who were now two glowing masses of light in front of me. I looked up with squinting eyes and thanked them for their blessing, raising my hands upwards with my palms facing outwards. Then closing my eyes once more, I thanked the Lady and Lord and told them to go in peace. One speaks this way after summing such powerful deities. It also serves that you have concluded your ritual. When I opened my eyes again, I could see the two bright lights fading away until there was no trace of their presence.

I traced the circle, which I had made with my index finger, this time, and moving counter- clockwise. I envisioned the energy seeping back into my finger again. Once completed, it was time to head off to work.

There was a big presentation today for a major pharmaceutical company that wanted some graphical stills done for their products, and guess who was responsible for delivering this presentation? Bruce Kirkpatrick our illustrious boss thought I would be perfect for the job.

Honestly, I think that ever since he learned of my Wiccan heritage, he has been trying to become my left arm so to speak in all things Wicca. He frequently visits my office and will sit for hours dragging me into conversation after conversation regarding Wiccan. I will never forget the day he came out of the Wiccan closet so to speak. You see no matter how much we prove otherwise, witches, both male, and female, still tend to receive a negative outlook by most people of other faiths. Therefore, when Bruce learned of my openness of being a witch, he came fourth and openly admitted it to me that he too, was a partitioning Wiccan. Ever since he has always made it a note to speak to me. You would think that I had bewitched him and not so much our clientele as he often jokingly states.

I proceeded to make my way downstairs just then; I heard the sound of papers frantically being flipped around. I glanced up the third flight of stairs, which lead to the attic. Ever since I could remember, Aunt Ellice and Uncle Adler have always kept that particular door locked but would never tell me why. I started up the third flight of stairs ending up in a tiny hallway where, at the very end, lay the attic door. The door gave the appearance of age and weakness but that was not the case. Once when my Aunt and Uncle were at a gathering, I attempted to force my way into the attic but kicking, and even ramming it but no such luck. Funny thing is that there is no visible lock of any kind on the door, just a carving of a pentagram with runic symbols surrounding it just above the door handle. I remember when I first attempted to touch the door at that spot; the shock of energy that came from it threw me a good three feet backward.

If it had been an inch more, I would have gone right down the stairs nonstop. Since that night, I have never tried to venture up to the attic, let alone touch that door. Nevertheless, what was that sound coming from behind the door? Well, no time to play detective. I had twenty minutes to drive downtown and get to work before the start of the presentation so this mystery, like the one I was already pondering regarding what had happened this morning, will just have to wait until the weekend. Descending the stairs as quickly as my legs would take me, I headed for the front door, saying goodbye as I exited the house.

As I entered my midnight blue Toyota Camry, I could hear the voices of Aunt Ellice and Uncle Adler responding with goodbyes of their own and blessed be. I hit the ignition, tapped the gas and off I went.

Although there are still some people who do not feel comfortable around Wiccans, a good number, most in high-ranking positions of office, have taken to the "Live and Let Live" stance. Ever since the Wicca Acknowledgment Act became law, there have been more shops, and even a radio station geared towards Wiccans. I enjoy listening to that station because they play a lot of Celtic music. WIC Radio are its call letters and I have become good friends with the station manager Richard Daniels. If there were a particular song that I would like to hear, all I need do is close my eyes, envision Richard's happy-go-lucky face and just send the title to him in thought. Next thing you know, I would hear the DJ on the radio say "And this next song is for the lovely Anora Rhianlugh from all of us at WIC radio."

Richard and I usually hang out at one of the Wiccan bars. He has long since granted me permission to telepathically communicate with him as long as I do not pry too deeply into his subconscious.

Although Richard is, in fact, a practicing witch, he lacks the ability to send thoughts telepathically, he can only receive, but sometimes, when our schedules permit, we would meet in the field near my home and work spells or meditate in order to help him along. The only reason I can even hold a conversation with him in this manner, is that I can hear his thoughts. Therefore, all he need do is think the response and I will respond back. It will suffice for now and we have even managed to have a bit of fun with it from time to time. I started to feel more energetic and refreshed now, perhaps due to the cool autumn air or the blessing, which the Lady and Lord had placed upon me earlier. Nevertheless, it felt good and I was going to utilize this as much as possible.

I arrived at the office building and entered the underground parking garage. Normally, it would be a task in itself to find a parking space here but that is just one of the benefits of being the Boss's star worker.

Only a select few are given their own parking space and lucky me, I happen to be one of them. I exited the car and entered the small glass room where the elevators were situated. I pressed the shiny steel button and was immediately greeted by a ding and the opening of the doors. I ascended to the twenty-third floor to where the offices of the GrafX Design Company, my home away from home.

I have always told Bruce that he could have chosen a more unique name for his company but he told me that the name sort of came to him while on his porcelain throne. I have never brought up the subject since learning that tidbit of unnecessary information. I wonder what other miraculous ideas were spawned while on his throne. Perhaps choosing me to give this presentation was one of them.

I walked through the thick glass doors and was greeted by Alicia Carrington, the company's receptionist and official enterprising person of all things caffeine related. She looked up with big blue eyes underneath thin black framed glasses. Her dark brown hair was up today and she was not wearing her signature ruby red lipstick.

"Ah good morning Anora, they're waiting for you in the conference room."
"Has the presentation started already?" I asked with a slight hint of surprise.
"I don't think so; the client hasn't even shown up yet."
"That's strange, it's after ten, and you'd think they'd be here on time if not earlier."

I made my way down the burgundy-carpeted hallway and past several offices until reaching my own. Opening the door, I entered the brightly lit room thanks to the glare of the sun and a very good size window. I placed my bag on the chair and thumbed through the mail that was waiting on my desk.

No sooner had I sat down in the large leather chair and turned on my computer to view my emails when who else but the boss himself Bruce Kirkpatrick entered, his face holding an expression of part happy to see me and part frustration. However, I doubt that the frustration was geared towards me.

"Hello Anora, and how are we this fine morning."

There was absolutely no way in hell I was going to mention the events, which took place earlier. After all, how could I even begin to word it? "Oh well, I was raped by someone using air magick on me." Yeah, I can just see the expression on his face. Therefore, I put together the events starting from sitting with Aunt Ellice and Uncle Adler up to now and summed it up in one sentence, which I hoped would satisfy him.

"Oh, I'm just peachy Bruce and yourself?"
"Well seeing that our ten o'clock hasn't shown up yet, I've been in better moods."
"Has there been any contact?" I asked trying to help calm him down.
"Well, Alicia received a call about five minutes ago from his personal assistant saying that they were on route and should arrive shortly. Now that would be fifteen minutes ago."

In my years of working for Bruce Kirkpatrick, I have come to learn that there are at least two major things which he has zero tolerance for, blatant displays of ignorance and tardiness.

I could see that this client was starting things off on a bad note with him. I stood up from my chair so that he could get a good look at all of me. The fact that I had long naturally copper hair was bad enough but add to that my slender frame and ample breasts which forced me to undo the top three buttons of my blouse, well that was more than enough to bring him to a calmer state of mind.

"Damnit Anora, no matter how upset I get all it seems to take to bring me around is a full glance of your lovely body."

"Well Bruce, you know that we can't have the head of the company upset especially at the beginning of the business day." I leaned over the desk and laid a hand on his face. As I looked into his eyes and smiled, I knew that his stare was more focused on my chest, but hey, I accomplished what I set out to do.

"Where would I be without you around to snap me back to reality?" He uttered still feeling the warmth of my hand and still gazing at the amount of cleavage I was presenting.

"Well, hopefully, we'll never have to find that out for quite some time."

"You know there are times when I wish I wasn't your boss?"

"Um, and why is that?" I asked but I already knew what he was going to say.

"Because then I could look at you in a much more intimate light."

"Now Bruce, I honestly don't think that a successful and handsome man like you would want to waste his time and efforts on a small suburban lady like me."

He placed his hand on mine, which was still against his face and turned his view up to meet my gaze. Either I must have touched a nerve or he actually contemplated that thought. Just then, Alicia entered the threshold of the office, stopping midpoint between the openings. She tapped lightly upon the class of the door attempting to get our attention. Bruce turned suddenly causing my hand to drop from his face. I remained behind my desk folding my arms across my chest. It was clear that Alicia thought she had interrupted an intimate moment, however, she did not quite understand the sort of relationship Bruce and I shared and I was not in the mood to explain it to her.

"Yes, Alicia what is it?" He said. His voice deepened to spark a sort of fear from her as if to say, "How dare you to interrupt."

"I'm sorry for intruding Mr. Kirkpatrick but your ten o'clock has arrived and is in the conference room along with the rest of the staff."

"Very well, tell them that we will be there shortly." He said still with that deep voice.

Immediately after instructing her to deliver the message, he called her again. Alicia turned suddenly and smiled.

"Yes, Mr. Kirkpatrick?"

"Just for the record Alicia, this wasn't what you may think it was understood?"

"Yes, Mr. Kirkpatrick I understand completely." She said turning again suddenly and walking more quickly down the hallway, the sounds of her footsteps suggest that Bruce was successful with instilling fear in her.

"You know Bruce you're going to frighten that poor girl to death one day."

"Well if they are going to fester rumors of us being intimate, at least, let them be true."

"Oh Bruce, I don't think you would be comfortable with how I like my lovemaking."

He turned to look at me and offered his hand. I placed my hand into his and allowed him to guide me from behind my desk and to the office door. Once under the threshold he stopped and turned me to face him, his eyes half opened.

"Ever since I've come to know you Anora, I've always wondered about your style of lovemaking and off the record, I'd welcome the opportunity."

"Well let's just say that as there are different planes of existence, I prefer sex on a plane other than this one."

"Still, I would love to experience it." His voice held a sort of sincerity, which I could not completely ignore. I leaned into him and kissed him gently allowing him to taste my lips.

"Perhaps one day, but for now, you have to put your commander and chief personality on and I have to put on my best game face."

We walked down the hallway saying nothing but I knew that he was still thinking of that possibility where he could have my body and spirit in a night of passion. I just do not think that he is able to handle himself in a plane other than this one, otherwise, I would consider it.

Chapter Three

Gavin McLellan was standing at one of the windows of the conference room with his personal assistant Silvia Blakely next to him. Sitting around the large half-circled conference table were my colleagues Craig, Murray, Croix, and Delia all of whom like me, were employed by Bruce as graphics designers and animators. Of the four, only Croix and Craig were fellow Wiccans from my community. In fact, Croix informed Bruce of my family's history. Like myself, Croix was also born into the Craft and is an active member of my Aunt and Uncle's coven. I sometimes cannot help but wonder just how much of our coven did Croix tell Bruce about because, after his confession, he was quick to take part in our initiation ritual. Maybe he told him that we usually perform our rituals skyclad or naked for those not familiar with Wiccan customs. After all, no matter how comfortable one maybe in their own skin, you cannot help but notice a nice body even during a ritual.

Bruce and I turned our looks towards Mr. McLellan who by now had placed us both in his sights. Gavin McLellan was a tall well-built man who prided himself on always looking his best. We have seen photos of him prior to this meeting and he was the picture of masculine perfection in everyone.

He stood at about six feet five inches tall and was of a light cappuccino brown complexion possibly due to good tanning and healthy genes. His hair was sandy blonde and very well groomed. Although he was wearing an expensive Gucci suit, you could still tell that he kept his body in the best of shape. He was clean-shaven which brought out the strong sculpted features of his face. His nose was a bit small for my taste but he had nice kissable looking lips, which, in my opinion, made up for it. His eyes, however, were what interested me. They were clear almost transparent looking with a faint ring of dark blue around them.

As I stood to assess things, he began to advance towards us with his right hand outstretched and a smile that showed clean straight teeth on his face.

"So this is the famous Anora Rhianlugh for whom I've heard so much about." He said offering his hand.
"I'm afraid you have me a somewhat of a disadvantage Mr. McLellan."
"Please call me Gavin, and it's a pleasure to finally meet you."

His hand clasped mine. Suddenly, a wave of heat ran through my body and I felt the heat starting to stimulate the intimate parts of my body as it rushed through me. The sensation caused me to let out a gasp. I looked at Gavin McLellan with wide eyes. His expression did not alter, he still wore that perfect smile and his eyes were fixed on mine. I started to lose touch with what was around me until I heard Bruce interrupt by touching my shoulder as he spoke to Gavin.

"I believe we have a presentation to show you." Said Bruce, who was still holding my shoulder to help me focus.
"Yes by all means proceed." Said, Gavin, as he released his hold on my hand and proceeded to walk over to an empty chair. As he sat down, his assistant Silvia stood behind his right side like a bodyguard.

Silvia was about five feet seven inches tall, taller than me of course but then again she was wearing one-inch heels. Her skin was an olive color and her eyes were a dark brown. She wore clear lip-gloss and light reddish eye shadow, possibly to compliment her reddish suit jacket and pants. Her hair was dark brown and in a ponytail. As she took her place behind Gavin's chair, she fixed angry eyes upon me.

I sat down in the main chair since I was the one drafted to give this presentation. Bruce sat to the left of me, which put Croix on my right side. I think the two men silently planned this perhaps for my protection or their benefit. Nevertheless, their presence on either side did make me feel more at ease. Bruce may not be very skilled in magick but I knew that Croix was. Croix was in fact what we refer to in our coven as a Wiccan warrior, someone who specialized in magick designed to defend against negative energies and evil entities.

Croix was also good at telepathy. As I begun to pass around the portfolios to everyone, Croix began speaking to me telepathically.

"Anora are you alright, I could have sworn I felt something just then."

"I'm not sure Croix but there's more to this Gavin McLellan then what he's currently showing us."

"Judging by his expression now, I think he's making the same assumption about us."

"What do you mean?" I asked while focusing my attention on the projector in from of me.

"Well, he looks as though he can either hear us or he senses that we're communicating telepathically."

"You don't suppose he hears us do you?"

"No, otherwise we'd know."

"Lady and Lord just get me through this presentation."

"Oh don't worry that pretty head Anora, I got you covered."

"Maybe so but I'd feel more at ease if Kiedan were here as well to back you up."

"Aren't I good enough for you?" He said showing a hint of a grin on his face, which told me he was merely kidding around and had not taken my request personally.

"Perhaps in bed but this is much different, let's just get this over with." I said as I powered on the projector.

The sound of a thick book closing filled the air from where Gavin McLellan was sitting. He had closed the portfolio and was sitting hands folded and smiling. Silvia stood holding both her position behind him and her hateful gaze towards me.

"Is there something the matter?" asked Bruce.

"Why not at all sir, I just feel that I've seen more than enough material to convince me that your talented staff is more than qualified to handle my graphical needs."

"We set up a slide presentation for your viewing as well."

"Once again there is no need, I'm completely convinced in your company's abilities especially those of Miss Rhianlugh." He was staring wide-eyed at me now.

We all looked at one another in shock then turned towards where Gavin McLellan was sitting. He had raised his left hand towards Silvia who then placed a leather bound checkbook into it.

"So if I'm not mistaken we agreed on five thousand dollars for the work?" he asked turning his gaze towards Bruce who had now begun to stand up.
"Yes that's correct and you're free to take the portfolio with you."

I could tell that Bruce was a bit annoyed at the actions of this man. First, he shows up fashionably late, now he cancels the presentation we worked so hard on. Gavin had risen from his seat causing Silvia to step back from her position behind him. He walked over smiling towards Bruce and handed him the check. Bruce paused for a moment, I guess to put his professional face back on before anyone noticed, then with a slight smile he took the check from the man and offered his hand.

"So this concludes our meeting then Mr. McLellan?" He said still holding his hand.
"Indeed Mr. Kirkpatrick, I look forward to future dealings as well but if you all would excuse me, I have other matters to attend to before the closing of the day." He said as he now shifted his gaze once more in my direction.
"And I look forward towards meeting you again Miss Rhianlugh."

He then walked out of the conference room with Silvia trailing behind him. When we heard the sound of Alicia wishing them a good day, we all began to stare at each other in astonishment at what had just transpired.

"Does someone want to tell me exactly what the hell that was all about?" Said Murray as he arose from his chair.
"I guess he'd seen all that he needed to see." I said shutting off the projector and standing from my chair as well.
"That is one arrogant son of a bitch." Said Bruce as he now showed us his full disgust for Mr. Gavin McLellan.

"Well, one thing for certain he's got eyes for you Anora." Said Delia who until now remained silent and possibly unaware of what happened when Gavin McLellan touched my hand earlier. She stood up from her chair and went on.

"Did you all see how hard he was looking at her? It was as if he were undressing her with his eyes of something."

"That's enough Delia; Anora is probably already uncomfortable as it is without you egging things on." Said Craig as he too rose from his chair and started towards the opened door. "Besides, it's about lunch time and I for one am famished."

I began to wonder to myself if this was not in fact, one of those days which I should have stayed in bed, or at least taken the advice of Uncle Adler and remained home. Clearly someone or something had some sort of an interest in me today but why? I walked out of the conference room and down the hall to my office door. I was so preoccupied with my thoughts that I had not noticed Croix following behind me. It was not until I had reached my desk and turned around when I saw him standing there. He had that look of concerned Samaritan on his face.

Croix was quite the looker; in fact, he had received several offers for modeling contracts in the past but turned them down. Croix was just five feet nine inches tall but what he lacked in height he made up for in body. He was always clean-shaven, his hair straight and flawless, not a strand out of place. He had dark brown eyes but changed when upset or sad to a light brown. His facial structure was equipped with high cheekbones and a strong jawline. I could attest that he had a perfect male body since he is part of my Aunt and Uncle's coven and, therefore, participated in all of our skyclad rituals. I started to think about his nude body under the light of the full moon. His skin was not as white as mine, but light enough to give it that glow when the moonlight danced upon it.

It was not until he started laughing that I regained my thoughts and looked at him with puzzled eyes.

"What's so funny?" I asked.
"You're having sexual thoughts about me again aren't you?"

"Were you reading my thoughts Croix?"

"Don't have to, it's written all over your pretty little face."

"Ok you got me but after this morning, I can't help but feel just a bit on the aroused side." I said with a bit of redness to my cheeks.

"This morning, what happened this morning?" He asked as he begins walking forwards, stopping inches away from me.

"Someone used air magick to try and rape me."

"What?" He yelled nearly falling backward from the force of his own word.

"If not for Aunt Ellice and Uncle Adler coming when they did, they probably would have succeeded." I said with a hint of a sigh as to doubt my own ability to protect myself.

"Do you know who it could be?" He asked but he already knew my response, I think he merely asked because he had nothing else to say.

"No, but Aunt Ellice an Uncle Adler are meeting with the other coven members to discuss it."

"Now it makes sense, I could feel that there was more on your mind than just the presentation this morning but I didn't want to pry."

I stepped towards him and laid a gentle kiss upon his lips. The taste of him stirred sensations deep inside my body and caused more intimate parts to awaken with pleasure. He took his arm and wrapped it around my waist pulling me closer into him, into the kiss itself. He began to probe my mouth with his tongue and I followed with the same gesture. I started to feel the heat of his aura against my skin, the waves of energy made the hairs on my arms stand up and my nibbles perk. He ran his hand down the length of my back stopping and squeezing the right side of my ass.

The sudden gesture brought out a soft moan from my lips and made me lay into the kiss with more intensity. The movement of our mouths became wilder with passion as he tried to invade my throat with his tongue. The sheer sensation once more brought a deep gasp from my mouth. I could feel the warmth of his aura brushing against mine. The combination of the mixture made both of our bodies shake. I quickly pulled back from the kiss only to stare into a pair of hungry looking eyes.

"What's wrong Anora?" He said with a combination of concern and disgust.

"Not here Croix and certainly not now, not after everything that's happened thus far."

"I understand and I'm sorry."

He lowered his head in shame for entertaining such primal urges and not thinking of my current emotional state. I touched his shoulder and kissed him.

"But that doesn't mean not ever." I said with a slight but seductive smile.

"Should I take that as an advanced invitation?" He said looking happier than before.

"What do my eyes tell you?" I said as I begun envisioning us making love underneath the night sky.

I brought images of our potential lovemaking to the surface of my eyes for him to see. He took a deep hard look for a few moments then smiled.

"I will be counting down the moments." He said as he continued to smile but now displaying a set of perfect teeth.

We stood face to face for a moment, trying to do our best to calm ourselves after that brief moment of passion. Croix looked at his watch then turned his gaze back towards me.

"Expecting someone Croix?" I asked.

"Not really, I have a clear schedule today and you?"

"Gavin McLellan was my only appointment because I didn't know how long the presentation would have lasted."

"Well, I'm thinking of going to the Bistro for lunch care to join me?"

"Let me check my email and I'll meet you in the receptionist area." I replied.

"Don't keep me waiting I don't know if I can handle waiting on you for both lunch and making love." He said jokingly as he walked out the door and down the hall to his office.

I sat down at my desk and turned towards the window. The sun was high and there was a nice blue sky to complement its radiance. No visible clouds as far as the eye could see, thus making it a picture perfect afternoon. I thought about going home to Aunt Ellice's cooking and some good meditation. I needed to sort some things out and take a cold shower to.

Croix was a fantastic lover and he had no problems with making love on different planes from time to time. We once made love near the famed mounds of Faerie but not before asking permission of course. The magick there made the act that much more intense and pleasurable. I do not believe that Bruce would be able to handle the magick which exists on other planes like Faerie, although, I am flattered by his willingness to make the attempt. However, if anything should happen to him, I do not think I could forgive myself. Although you can have a lot of fun on other planes, like anything else, there are dangers as well. Faeries, for instance, have a natural dislike for humans mostly because humans seem to destroy everything around them. It is only because of my Wiccan ancestry that the Fae folk allow my family and others like us to communicate with them. They also appreciate the fact that we practice our rituals nude. I do not think that Bruce is ready for such encounters yet although again, I admire his willingness to make the effort.

My heart was still racing from the kiss with Croix and although I wanted to go further, I did not quite feel that now was the time. I turned back to my desk, to my computer and proceeded to access my email. Inside my inbox was a message entitled A Fascinating Lady with none other than Gavin McLellan as the sender. It was company procedure to supply the business email addresses to clients in case they needed to contact us with last minute changes, but judging by the title, this was not such an email and I was hesitant to open it.

"What could he want so soon after meeting with him?" I thought to myself as I began sliding the cursor on the message to open it. I sat with a blank expression upon my face as I read his message.

Dear Miss Rhianlugh

       I am so glad to have finally met you after hearing so much praise. I am confident that your work will far exceed my expectations, but I am already impressed as to the amount of power that you seem to possess. I will not soon forget the brief exchange of energies between us. Perhaps you would honor me with a more in-depth demonstration. Until next time, we meet.

Blessed Be
Gavin McLellan

      Now this had to be the icing on the proverbial cake. I have never met this man until today and yet he speaks as though he has known me for years. In addition, he seems a bit fascinated in that brief exchange of energies when our hands touched. I wonder if he received the same sexual sensation as I did.

      Perhaps I was just reading too deeply into what could clearly be taken as the words of a rich playboy trying to flatter a woman into his bed. I moved the email to my personal folder and powered down the computer. I was done for the day and after having lunch with Croix, I decided to head back home. This was truly one of those rare days indeed and although I was hoping that the level of strangeness would decrease, I could not help but have my doubts. Lady and Lord help me for no matter how much I wanted this day to have a quiet ending, I felt that what has happened so far was merely the prelude to what was yet to come.

Chapter Four

Croix seemed to know that there was a new worry on my mind.
He gave that wanting to know what I was thinking stare but did not
want to pry. I wanted to tell him about the email sent by Gavin
McLellan but he had other more pressing things to concern himself
with. Being a Wiccan warrior was our community's equivalent to a
police officer except instead of firearms they carried talismans and
possessed knowledge of a variety of spells and incantations. Not to
mention their individual mental and physical capabilities.

Normally Wiccans believe in a simple rule "If it harms none
then do as you will." However, there have been times throughout our
history when we had to defend ourselves not just from other humans
but also on occasion, other beings. Our Wiccan warriors or as we have
come to call them the Celtic Knights were made up of some of the
most powerful men and women in our community. Their job was to
defend the community from such attacks. They are the front line of
defense in all matters both natural as well as supernatural.

Croix was one of our most powerful Celtic Knights. He always
practices his mental talents and spell casting. It also stands to mention
that his family like my own have been practitioners of the Craft for
centuries. Now he was trying to be my personal therapist.

"Ok Anora, now what's on your mind?" He asked.
"Just what I've already told you Croix." I replied trying to keep
the thought of that email from Gavin McLellan out of my head.
"You know I cannot help you if you won't let me."
"I know but you have more to tend to than my problems." I
could sense that he was trying to bait me into telling him.
"Well again I won't pry but don't forget I'm willing to help you
when you need it." He said as he took a sip of his tea.
"I know Croix and I do love you for it but I don't think it's such
a big issue."

"Are you kidding me?" He yelled nearly spilling his tea in the process.

"You were sexually assaulted by someone using air magick no less, not to mention that little episode with Gavin McLellan in the conference room and you say it's not a big deal?"

I did not want to fight with him on this but then again he was sort of right. Perhaps I was not taking this as seriously as I should but I was tired from all the activity and I really wanted to just go home and soak in a nice warm tub. I took a sip of my tea and closed my eyes, trying to put myself in the fields behind my house or perhaps the woods near the Faerie mounds, anywhere other than where I was right now. Was I trying to run? All I knew was I needed time to myself and I was not getting it in the present company.

"I think I'm going to call it a day Croix, after all, it's slow and we don't have to start the McLellan project until next week."

"Yes by all means Anora go home and rest." "I shall look in on you when I get back." He said as he finished his tea.

"Will you be at the initiation ceremony tonight?" He asked with that look of hope in his eyes. "You know we have a few new members joining."

"I will be there Croix don't worry."

"Good then it's a date." He smiled sheepishly when he said it.

"Sure as long as you don't mind the rest of the coven attending."

"Touché Anora."

We both stood up and left the table. As I started back towards the office parking lot, I felt something brush against my right ear. It was the wind but there were words carried on it and I heard them as clearly, as if they were being spoken right in front of me. That sudden feeling caused me to stop dead in mid walk.

"I look forward to seeing you again Anora for you fascinate me so." It said.

"Who are you?" I asked not realizing how loud I had said it.

"I have tasted you already and just the mere taste of you has caused such a longing for more."

"Who the hell are you?" This time, I said it so loudly that Croix ran over to see whom I was yelling to.

"Anora who are you talking to?" He asked.

"I think it's the same son of a bitch who used air magick to rape me."

"May I read your thoughts?" He asked grabbing my hand in the process.

"You want to ease drop don't you?" I replied.

"Yes."

"Sure." I replied.

Croix clutched my hand and closed his eyes. Within moments, I could feel his presence inside my head. I envisioned him sitting quietly in a corner of my mind listening to the conversation that was taking place.

"Talk to him." He whispered.

"So why won't you tell me who you are?" I asked.

"You will find out soon enough pretty lady for you and I will soon make history."

"What do you mean by that?"

"All in due time, besides there are too many ears listening."

Croix opened his eyes and stared at me with such surprise that you would have thought he had just won a game show.

"Shit, how did he sense that I was listening?" He said with wonderment.

"I don't know but it's clear that whoever he is, he's very powerful." I replied letting out a small sigh after I said it.

We both stood motionless, wondering what was to come in the near future. One thing was certain, whoever this person is, he is very skilled in magick and he has his sights set on me. I really needed to get home now more the ever and see what Aunt Ellice and Uncle Adler have to say.

"We need to get you somewhere safe Anora."

"That's why I'm going home." I replied.

"Here take this it will help shield you until you can get yourself situated."

He reached into his coat pocket and handed me a small purple pouch. Inside was a tiger's eye stone on a gold chain. The stone looked so shiny and bright in the light. I placed the charm around my neck. When it touched my skin, a warm jolt of energy streaked through my body causing me to shiver slightly. My eyes began to tingle with energy and I let out a sharp gasp.

"That's interesting." Croix said.
"What?" I replied.
"It's never reacted in that way before." "It's as if you set it off or something."
"I don't know how I could have done that Croix." I said with a look of confusion on my face.

The charm was warm in my hand, it flared up with energy, this time, it came in sharp waves that ran from head to toe. The sensation made me throw my head back and moan as the waves continued to run downward hitting my body with energy.

Croix grabbed me from behind before I fell over. When he touched me, the waves passed into him causing him to temporarily lose his footing. We both leaned against a nearby wall as the waves proceeded to run through us. The feeling of warm energy hitting my tender spots made me moan more until I could no long hold the climax that it had brought forth in me. I felt myself growing wet from the sensation and I could not stop it. I cried out in pure pleasure and stood against the wall with my head down, my hair covering my face. The waves steadily subsided and stopped. Croix cautiously touched my shoulder.

"Anora are you alright?"
"Yes, I think so." I said in a soft tone. I had not fully regained my composure and still relied on the sturdiness of the wall.
"What in the name of the God and Goddess was that?" He asked but I knew he just wanted to hear me say it so I obliged him.
"I had an orgasm thanks to the energy from the tiger's eye."

"From the looks of it, it must have been a mind-shattering one."

"It was." I said making sure not to draw any attention to the stain below.

"I need to get home." I continued as I stood up and removed my jacket to wrap around my waist making sure it covered the stain. I started walking towards the back of the office building taking slow steps until I fully regained my stability.

Croix walked alongside me making sure not to touch me but ready to assist if needed. The tiger's eye rested against my skin. Although it was still warm with energy, it no longer sent those rushing waves through my body. Thank the Lady and Lord of that. I do not think I could take another mind-blowing orgasm like that right now and especially not in front of Croix. We finally reached the underground parking lot and made our way towards where I had parked. The air was cool from the central air conditioning but it was not cold enough to bring about a chill. I reached my car and opened the door to get in when Croix took my hand and turned me towards him. He had that look of concern on his face again and I knew that nothing I could say would ease him after what he had just witnessed.

"Look Anora." He started but was interrupted by the placing of my fingers to his lips.

"I know what you're going to say Croix and I cannot say anything which will ease your conscious." "All I can say is that I promise to go straight home."

"That will suffice then." He said releasing my hand so I could get into the car.

"I'll see you tonight at the initiation ceremony." I continued as I closed the door and started the engine.

"As I said before, it's a date."

I pulled off leaving him standing there with his hands on his sides. I felt better now and was able to focus again but I had yet another thing to figure out. Lady and Lord help me,

Perry Mason I am not and here I am faced with these questions. I needed something to ease my nerves.

As I exited the underground parking lot and onto the street, I turned on the radio and started to concentrate on my good friend Richard. I envisioned his smiling face in my mind as I silently spoke.

"Merry Meet Richard, I need something upbeat for the ride home if you please."

I waited a few moments then repeated the phrase once more. Just then, a voice echoed in my head loud and joyful as Richard responded to my request.

"Hey, Anora always a pleasure to hear from you pretty lady what do you want to hear?"
"No preference as long as it's upbeat." I said.
"You got it sweetie and don't be a stranger you hear?"
"I promise." I said as I broke the connection and focused on the road.

Just as it has always been, when I communicate with Richard, and make a request, he instructs the DJ on duty to play it and I hear my request fulfilled. It is nice to be treated like a celebrity sometimes. Richard was true to his word and played something Celtic and upbeat for the ride home. I quickly thanked him and told him that I owed him a kiss when I see him next. I am sure he will hold me to it. Lady and Lord willing, I will get home without any more incidents.

Chapter Five

"Home sweet home." I muttered to myself as I started to feel the protective energies that surrounded our little town. The powers of the spell seemed much stronger than when I had left this morning, which told me that whatever Aunt Ellice and Uncle Adler had said to the rest of the members, was taken seriously. I wanted to find out what transpired but first things first, I need a shower and a change of clothes. I pulled up next to the house and proceeded inside. The house still smelled of Aunt Ellice's muffins but there was another smell present. The second aroma was the type of smell that would cause you to envision a clear sunny day in October when autumn's kiss touches the land along with the fresh smell of falling leaves. One cannot help but think of happier times when they come across such a scent.

I ascended upstairs and straight to the bathroom removing all my clothes in the process. As the water ran in the tub, I thought of what had happened recently, as if I needed anything else to think about today. I remembered the feeling that the tiger's eye gave me when it first touched my skin.

I recalled the waves upon waves of energy that raced through my body bringing out the woman in me. I thought about how it felt when I touched Gavin McLellan's hand at the presentation, and how it felt when Croix kissed me. All of these sensations caused things low inside of me to swell and contract with pleasure. It was as if I were bewitched by the mere thought of it all. I turned off the faucet and climbed into the warm, bubbly goodness of the tub.

I imagined the water washing away all of the negative energy that had attached itself to my body. I pictured the God and Goddess bestowing their blessings upon me this morning and I began to drift away into myself. The walls of the bathroom started to disappear and suddenly I was in a meadow of fresh smelling grass accompanied by tall strong trees.

I could smell the sweet flowers, which swayed back and forth in the cool breeze. As I stared out at the vast land, I heard a voice calling to me from the distance. It was faint and soft but I could not yet make out the gender.

As I continued to look out at the vast meadow before me, I could feel the magick that the land held within. It seemed to rise from the bottom of the earth and slowly upwards towards the sky, touching everything in its path with its warmth. I was being showered in it. All the magick, all the beauty of the land just seemed to entrance me. I could still hear the voice calling out to me from the distance but now it appeared that it was closer than before.

I realized that it was masculine in nature but I still could not see a figure. I started wondering who was calling me and why wouldn't they reveal themselves?

"Anora." It said echoing through my head like a thunderous applause.

I still could not see a figure but I did feel something pressing on my left shoulder. The pressure made me realize that it was an invisible hand trying to grip my shoulder. As it continued to grip me, the voice grew closer and its call to me, more constant. Even when I responded, it just continued repeating my name while the hand held fast to my shoulder but now it felt as if it were trying to pull me but to where? Suddenly as instantly as the meadow had appeared so too did it vanish. The sweet autumn smell was gone and there was a weight pressed against my chest now. Another smaller hand held now joined the first, and had gripped my right shoulder. The next thing I knew, I was in the tub being supported by the hands of Aunt Ellice and Uncle Adler.

"Anora are you alright you nearly drowned." Said Aunt Ellice, her voice was high-pitched and frantic.
"I remember getting into the tub then the next thing I knew I was in a vast meadow." I said in a soft throaty tone. I had not completely come back from wherever I was.
"Apparently you somehow astral projected to another plane." Explained Uncle Adler as he continued his hold on my left shoulder.

"But I wasn't even concentrating and I didn't feel myself leave my body."

"It appears there are more powerful. Magicks at work here." Said Uncle Adler his voice held a low tone, which meant he was beginning to worry.

"Finish your bath dear we'll talk more after you're done." Said Aunt Ellice as she attempted to soothe both Uncle Adler's spirits and mine.

They released their hold on my shoulders simultaneously and left the room. I sat there in the now lukewarm water trying to figure out what had happened. Had I somehow cause myself to astral project? Moreover, where did I go? At least, I figured out that the voice I heard were that of Uncle Adler calling to me. I could not take much more of this without some hint of an idea as to what was going on.

After my non-relaxing bath, I threw on some casual clothes and headed downstairs. Aunt Ellice and Uncle Adler were now outside on the wrap around porch. As I approached the front door, I could hear a second set of voices. I stopped just short of the front door and listened to see if I could determine whom the second set of voices belonged to. The second male voice was Croix. I should have known he would be by to see if I was all right. His voice sounded frantic and upset which led me to believe that he had been informed of my latest incident. The other voice was a bit more difficult to place, probably because whoever it was, did not talk as much as the others.

Finally, when the voice did speak I could tell that it belonged to a female. I decided to just go outside and see for myself since I was not sure. I could not rely on my powers of intuition right now. As I stepped out onto the wide wrap around porch, I could felt the sun's rays upon my skin. I closed my eyes for a moment and envisioned drinking in the warm energy that was being radiated upon me.

A hush immediately fell among the small group. Even with my eyes closed I could sense that they were staring at me, wondering what, if anything, was about to occur. I kept my eyes closed still concentrating on taking in the warmth from the sun. My body started tingling with the sensation of it filling me up inside.

From my toes upward, the heat rose higher until it reached my eyes. I felt the burning underneath my eyelids but I did not flinch, I just continued until it reached the very top of my head then slowly, I opened my eyes to gaze at my spectators.

Aunt Ellice, Uncle Adler, Croix and the fourth voice who I could now identify as Gretchen Wilkes, greeted me. Gretchen Wilkes was one of the elders in our coven. She also was one of the most powerful practitioners of the Craft. Gretchen is roughly two hundred and thirty-eight years old. Rumor has it that one day when she was younger she ventured into the woods to commune with nature, when she heard what she thought was a young girl screaming. She followed the cries until she came upon a small clearing where she found a woman stretched over a large rock by two hooded men. Gretchen called out to the two figures, who then turned and charged towards her.

It is also said that by her mental abilities alone, she managed to force their limbs to stop functioning thereby paralyzing them. As they fell to lay on the leaf-covered earth, she removed her cloak and gave it to the young woman.

The young woman stricken with fright ran off without so much as a thank you. Several months later Gretchen was once again in the woods when none other than the woman she had aided months earlier greeted her. With cloak in hand, the young woman offered it to her along with a fig leaf. Gretchen accepted both gifts and when she asked about the properties of the fig leaf, the young woman simply said that it would preserve her goodness for as long as that goodness is untainted by evil, and only then will she cease to exist. Ever since Gretchen consumed that fig leaf, she has escaped the hand of Death. Supposedly, that young woman was a faerie who rewarded Gretchen for her actions months before. Gretchen still treks through the woods and on occasion, has encountered the Wee Ones, but they merely flutter about and disappear when she tries to venture closer.

Gretchen Wilkes encounter with the famed Hidden People was not the first nor the last time one of us has crossed paths with them. Aunt Ellice has told me stories of times when even she has seen and talked with them.

It is one of the reasons why so many of the other covens have try to join us. It would seem that our coven is the only one for whom the Faeries trust and will render aid to if needed. Gretchen eventually broke the silence and walked over towards me.

"My dear child, are you alright?" She asked with one hand pressed upon my right shoulder.

"Yes, for the most part, I am thank you." I replied but I was not all right I was still a little out of phase with reality and I had more questions and even fewer answers.

"Your Aunt has just informed us that you were taken to another plane against your will." Said Croix. He was standing next to the white railing that stretched around the porch. He had his signature black jeans, black leather boots and dark blue cotton shirt on which meant he was getting ready for the initiation ritual when he learned of what had happened.

"Why aren't you with the other Celtic Knights preparing for tonight's initiation ceremony?"

"I was on my way there when I decided to look in on you especially after what happened this morning." He said which reminded me of the previous events that took place as well as what had just occurred in the bathroom.

"It was then when we learned of what had happened to you, my dear." Said Gretchen who was still holding my shoulder and staring at me with a look of wonderment in her eyes. I noticed the others had similar expressions on their faces.
"Is there something wrong? You're all staring at me funny." I pointed out.

"Anora your skin and eyes are glowing." Said Aunt Ellice, with a hint of shock in her voice.

Gretchen reached into her large bag and handed me a compact mirror. I opened it and looked at my reflection in the shiny clean glass. To my shock, they were right. My skin was lighter than usual and the whites of my eyes seem to complement the glow of the rest of my body. There were now two blackened spheres inside my eyes which if not for the bluish green ring would have appeared that there were two holes where my eyeballs should have been.

I closed the compact and gave it back to Gretchen who took and placed it back into her bag with her free hand.

"What does this mean?" I asked hoping that someone among the four would step up and provide the much-desired answer.

"You're special just as I have been telling you all these years dear." Shouted Aunt Ellice. She seemed pleased with herself at the thought that perhaps she was, in fact, right.

"You must attend tonight's ritual dear." Demanded Gretchen who finally removed her hold on my shoulder and started to make her way down the wooden steps of the porch and onto the dirt road. She turned for a moment and gazed up at me once more.

"I have reason to believe that your Aunt is correct in her assumption of you but we will know more come tonight's ceremony."

"I had best be going myself." Said Croix as he bowed his head, walked off the porch and followed Gretchen down the dirt road.

Clearly, someone had an idea of what was going on and I was willing to bet that it was Gretchen Wilkes. Nevertheless, why was she hiding it from me? I enjoy a good surprise as much as the next person but this was not the time for such a gala thing as that. I needed to know who or what was behind these "attacks" and why am I the target? I could see that I was not going to get any answers at this moment so I composed myself and turned my stare towards Aunt Ellice and Uncle Adler who were standing at the edge of the porch watching Gretchen and Croix walk down the path and out of sight.

"I don't suppose you know anything?" I asked the two of them as they stood with their backs towards me.
"Please if you know something tell me, this is happening to me so why should I be the last to know?"

Aunt Ellice lowered her head then turned to face me while Uncle Adler turned and walked over. He placed a gentle kiss on my forehead then departed down the wooden steps and along the dirt road in the same direction as Gretchen and Croix. I was now left staring at Aunt Ellice, as she stood ashamed, her long hair covering her face until finally she raised it to look at me.

"Please sit down Anora." She said as she took a seat on the white wooden bench.

"Aunt Ellice what's wrong?" I asked as I sat next to her. Her hands were resting on her lap one on top of the other. I laid my hands on hers in support. I could tell that whatever she was about to divulge was not going to be easy for her.

"Aunt Ellice what's wrong?"

"Three days ago we received word that someone had stolen a sacred Grimoire from a neighboring coven." She said.

"Do they know who it was?"

"They said that prior to the theft, a woman wandered in seeking food and shelter. The coven took her in and when they checked on her the next day, she and the Grimoire were gone."

"Which grimoire was it that was taken?" I asked although something told me whichever one she named was not going to be a good one.

"The thief took the Grand grimoire the one which we vowed to keep hidden for its pages contain the text to bring about the coming of the Old Ones."

Aunt Ellice's hands began to tremble beneath mine after she said that. I could not blame her for whom ever deciphers the text in that book can work all sorts of elemental magick as well as summoning both light and dark entities to do their will. Let us not forget the summoning of the Old Ones themselves. This news did not sit well with me. Whoever took the book apparently knows how to decipher it and could be using it to target me. However, there is that other question which I am still struggling with, why me? Then it occurred to me that it was exactly three days ago when I started having those dreams.

"It's starting to make sense now." I said to her still trying to calm her down by stroking her hands.

"What does Anora/"

"It was three days ago when I started having those dreams or visions as you care to call them." "Add to that the events which took place this morning and there you have it."

"Have what child?" "You're starting to not make sense."

"This woman has obviously deciphered the text and for some reason decided to target me."

"I fear it's much more than that my dear." She said with a sigh.

"What do you mean Aunt Ellice?"

"I'm afraid that whoever this person is, they are attempting to resurrect the Old Ones, and they either view you as a threat or an asset."

"What?" I said nearly falling from my seat. My hands flung from atop of Aunt Ellice's lap and ended up pressed to the sides of my now horrified face.

"Me a threat or an asset how can they view me as either?" I asked.

"Well my dear I have told you time and again that you're special, it's safe to assume that this person believes it as well."

"But Aunt Ellice I'm not special I'm just me."

"Oh, my sweet child you were special since birth." She said now looking into my eyes slightly smiling.

"Aunt Ellice if you know something that can help shed some light on all this I'm begging you please tell me."

"For starters, your mother went into labor on Hollow's Eve."

"Yes, I know hence my birthday." I said unconsciously sounding smug about it. Nevertheless, I wanted to know something that I was not already aware of and I was trying to remain patient.

"Perhaps, but what you don't know my child are the circumstances which surrounded your birth."

"And what circumstances were those?"

"I'm sorry child but I can't get into it at this moment." She said as she rose from her seat and walked off the porch and down the road.

I was now alone on the porch, still seated on the white wooden bench, wondering what in the hell was going on. Two things were now clear. First, the woman who stole the Grand Grimoire was the one responsible for the attacks on me and second, it was clear that Aunt Ellice, Uncle Adler, and Gretchen Wilkes knew more than what they were willing to tell me. Nevertheless, why are they keeping me in the dark when it is obvious that all of this seems to have something to do with me?

Are they merely trying to protect me from whatever or whomever it is that wishes me harm or is there more to it than that? Damnit I hate being kept in the dark but neither Aunt Ellice nor Uncle Adler would keep anything from me without a damn good reason, and that is what frightens me. Well, there is no sense in sitting around wondering. After all, I have an initiation ceremony to attend. I wondered whom it was they are initiating. Great another unanswered question but, at least, I will learn the answer to this one soon.

It was seven o'clock and everyone in the town had gathered in the field behind the hall. The hall itself was decorated in the theme of the season. The walls were draped with vines containing pretty green and light brown leaves along with an assortment of flowers ranging from white daisies to purple lilies. The altar was adorned with all the ritualistic tools of the Craft. Large sixteen-inch statues of the Goddess and the God were present, each with small white candles in from of them arranged in a circular pattern.

There were two incense burners, one made from the bark of an old oak tree, the other made of brass. The chalice and bowls were of pure sterling silver each displaying carvings of the four elements. Underneath that entire decor was a large altar cloth of pure cotton with the triple moon design in gold on each side and the tree of life in green in the middle. Everything looked picture perfect and the smell of fresh leaves, grass, and assorted scented candles filled the air. It was outside where the ceremony would take place.

Further, behind the hall, sat a large clearing with a fountain positioned to the far left side and a large tree on the right. In the middle of the two stood two long tables both with white tablecloths over them protecting the contents underneath from bugs. Underneath were foods of all types, prepared by some of the coven members who were skilled in the kitchen. We do not refer to them as chefs, but more so as Kitchen Witches. Even through the covering, you could still smell cakes and bread as well as some steamed vegetables. I could even smell Aunt Ellice's muffins amidst the various fragrances.

Most of the people were dressed in dark loose fitting pants and shirts but everyone wore a cloak of their favorite color.

I was dressed in midnight blue pants with a matching dark blue blouse that had a plunging yet tasteful V-neck line.

Because we were having the actual initiation ceremony in the field, I wore my black flat shoes and my midnight blue cloak completed my attire. There were people conversing with one another and others who were partaking in a quick pre-ritual meditation. As I looked around, I noticed a hooded figure in white standing next to Uncle Adler and Croix. It is a rule in our coven that until your initiation is complete, you must wear a cloak of pure white to mark the beginning of your journey into the Craft as well as the coven. Only the Celtic Knights wore matching cloaks of black with a golden Celtic cross on the back.

I decided to go and introduce myself to this new initiate since there was not much else to do until the ceremony. As I walked up to the trio I heard Croix's voice inside my head. He sounded astounded and in near shock when his words echoed in my head.

"Anora you don't want to come any closer." He said to me
"Why not?"
"Because you won't believe who the new initiate is." He continued while making hand gestures to the others so as not to seem suspicious.
"Who is it?" I asked still walking towards the group.

The newcomer was standing with their back facing me so they could not see me approaching and the others gave no hint as to my pending arrival. I heard Croix say the word "its" in my head when suddenly the person in the white cloak turned around, simultaneously removing their hood. What happened to me next was sheer unadulterated shock.

"Hello, again Miss Rhianlugh so nice to see you again." Said Gavin McLellan with a smile.

I stopped suddenly. My throat felt as if it were closing in upon itself crushing any words, which tried to pass through. My mouth slightly opened and my eyes were wide with surprise.

The memories of our first encounter began playing in my mind like a repetitive movie clip. As he began to fill the space between us, I noticed that I was losing my balance. My legs were having difficulty supporting the rest of my body and I felt every muscle in my body vibrating. I tried to take in some of the fresh crisp night air in the hopes that it would stabilize me but it was no use, my throat was not letting anything out or in. I forced my widened eyes to blink several times in the hopes of snapping me out of this state I was in.

I realized only moments before he was in breathing distance of me that I was trembling but was it out of shyness or out of fright. I could feel the presence of both emotions. I desperately tried to compose myself so I blinked several more times and willed my throat to let in some fresh air. The sudden intake caused a noticeable rise in my chest, which I am sure both Gavin and Croix, took full advantage of the opportunity to glance at my breasts.

"Mr. McLellan what an unexpected surprise." I said attempting to put on my best poker face but I was never good at the actual game so I doubt that I was very effective. However, it appeared that no one either noticed or cared.

"I've so much anticipated our meeting again Miss Rhianlugh and you could only imagine my surprise when I learned that the coven I would be joining was, in fact, the very one in which you were a part of."

"Yes, what a coincidence." I said as my throat had finally begun to allow air to travel.

"I've heard nothing but good and interesting things about you Miss Rhianlugh."

"Thank you very much, Mr. McLellan."

"Please, we're soon to be brother and sister in Wicca, no need for formalities, call me Gavin." He said smiling a flash of straight white teeth.

"Alright, Mr. McLellan I mean Gavin." I said fighting to get his first name out of my mouth.

"And may I call you Anora?" He said.

"Sure."

"Splendid, I cannot wait to witness the power of this coven." "I have asked around for a coven in which I could obtain the most learning and I was directed here."

"Who directed you to us?" Asked Croix with a voice that made you think he was interrogating Gavin.

"Why your neighboring covens of course."

"Is that so?" Replied Croix, still with the interrogating voice.

"I've conducted interviews with various members from other covens and inquired as to where would one stand to gain the most knowledge and enlightenment." Said Gavin.

"I see?" Replied Gretchen Wilkes who had now taken residence next to Gavin.

"Indeed dear lady, I was told that some of the most powerful Wiccans reside here and if one such as myself wishes to learn the Craft to its fullest then here is where I ought to be wouldn't you agree Anora?"

"Um yes, I would imagine so." I said scattering to find the words. I was not comfortable standing so close to him but I had to maintain pretenses at least for the moment. After all, from what he's said thus far, it seems he's looking to be trained in the Craft which would put him in the hands of one of our eldest members such as Gretchen Wilkes so there wouldn't be many confrontations between he and I except for the rituals of the Sabbats and of course any future initiation ceremonies.

"Well, I do so look forward to seeing all that your coven has to offer." He continued

"You are new to our coven but are you also new to the Craft?" I asked taking the same interrogating tone as Croix.

"Oh, I've been actively partaking in it every chance I get." He replied his gleaming smile now turned to a grin with no showing of teeth.

Aunt Ellice touched Gretchen Wilkes on her left shoulder causing her to focus her attention onto her. Uncle Adler and Croix both had begun walking towards the altar.

"Gretchen we are ready to proceed with the ceremony." She said still holding onto Gretchen's shoulder and looking happily at Gavin McLellan and me.

"Yes, you are so right Ellice. It's time ladies and gentleman." Said Gretchen Wilkes.

"Well, I guess I'll see you later Anora." Said Gavin as he placed his hood on his head and walked with Gretchen Wilkes to the outdoor altar.

I stood there looking around at all who were now gathering for tonight's ceremony and started wondering what was going to happen next. I remembered the strange sensation I felt when I touched Gavin's hand at the office and now here he is practically at my front door. I could not help but wonder if Gavin's arrival here was not just a happenstance. There was something going on here and I needed to get on the ball and figure this out before I end up having yet another episode.

Something about Gavin McLellan did not sit well with me. Perhaps I am just being paranoid and it is just a simple thing like a man's hormonal interest in me. Now that I can handle, but what if it is more than that? What if what I am feeling about him goes deeper than just a man's obsession? Well, nevertheless, I can't stop what's about to occur simply cause I'm having bad vibes about the man. The fact remains that he is a client with the design firm, which I work for and shortly he will become a member of the coven, which I belong to. This man seems to be fortifying himself in just about every aspect of my life and that bothers me.

We all gathered near the altar as Gavin stood in-between Gretchen Wilkes and Aunt Ellice with Uncle Adler next to her. Standing in pairs of three
on both sides of the foursome were the members of the Celtic Knights. The many tiny stars floating overhead lighted the night sky. The air was warm and carried the smell of fresh flowers in it.

As Gretchen commenced with the introductory proceedings, I closed my eyes and concentrated on Croix. I wanted to talk with him and I envisioned him hearing me.

"Croix can you hear me?"
"Loud and clear beautiful, what can I do for you?"

"I can't place it but I'm getting a strange feeling from our Mr. McLellan."

"I share in your intuition Anora but all we can do is wait and see what his true intentions are."

"Hopefully, by that time, it won't be too late." I replied.

Chapter Six

We all gathered around the altar for the start of the ritual. Aunt Ellice and Uncle Adler were standing on one side of the large altar while Gretchen and Jason Willerby, who were the alternate High Priest and Priestess, stood on the other side. Because of the strange sensation that I was feeling at the presence of Gavin McLellan, I did not want to be without someone I could count on beside me. I was lucky that this ceremony did not require the Celtic Knights to stand in their usual formation at the altar so I placed myself in-between Croix and Kiedan. Kiedan was just as tall as Croix but a little more muscular. His chest was broad and tight and he was one of the several men in our town who possessed a complete six-pack. His brown complexion reminded me of freshly dipped chocolate but smoother to the touch. I had a familiarity with him because we both had those haunting eyes with the exception of the bluish green rings around mine. There was not a single hair atop his head to speak of. As long as I can remember, Kiedan never had hair.

Kiedan was one of two individuals in our town who adorned such a dark complexion. The other was his twin brother Tiegan who except for the thin beard under his chin was the spitting image of Kiedan. Aunt Ellice once told me that Kiedan and Tiegan were the result of their mother being sacrificed to a demon and was impregnated so as to carry on his seed in this plane.

However, their mother did not want them to follow the path of their demonic father and thus, she fled her village and came here. The trip cost her, her life but she left the twins in the care of our elders who raised them to be Celtic Knights. Both Kiedan and Tiegan possess psychical strength and speed. Kiedan can shape shift which was a trait of their father, were as Tiegan inherited their mother's ability to control the elements. I liked talking to Tiegan at times because he was the most humorous of the two.

The area, which encircled the altar, was illuminated with candles and torches. The air was still now as Uncle Adler began to introduce Gavin McLellan to the rest of the coven members. Gavin was standing in-between Aunt Ellice and Uncle Adler with his white hooded cloak covering his head, his fingers folded in front of his body. I could not see his face but I could feel him exploring my most intimate of body parts with his thoughts. The feeling caused me to let out a gasp that caught the attention of both Croix and Kiedan.

"Anora are you feeling alright?" Kiedan asked in a low whisper.
"I'm not sure Kiedan but I can't help feeling that someone is watching me with hungry eyes."
"Well, Anora you know you're not exactly bad on the eyes." Replied Croix with a slight hint of a smile on his face.
"Normal stares I can handle but this is different, it's as if someone is peeling off my clothes and probing my most intimate parts with their eyes."
"That's an interesting analogy." Replied Croix closing his eyes perhaps in an attempt to visualize what I had just described.
"Perhaps but at the moment, it's quite unnerving."
"Well, can you sense who it might be?" Asked Kiedan still using his low whispering voice.
"If I didn't know better, I'd swear it was Gavin McLellan."
"I think it best that you stay near us for the time being Anora." Replied Croix, who was also using a low whispering tone.
"Well, you don't have to tell me twice."

The three of us stood watching the ceremony commence. They were introducing Gavin McLellan to the rest of the coven members and allowing him to say a few welcoming words before the actual initiation began. I could still feel a light breeze hitting my body every now and then as if to test the strength of my aura. I took a second to glance around the area for anything that I would have considered out of the ordinary. As far as I could see, there was nothing strangely out of place except for a large raven perched atop one of the trees, which encircled us. Just an ordinary raven I thought to myself but when I looked at it again, it seemed to look back at me with anger in its eyes.

At that moment, Kiedan raised his head to the sky and sniffed several times. He looked around and sniffed some more as if he were trying to catch the scent of something or someone.

"What's wrong Kiedan?" I asked.
"I think there's another shapeshifter close by."
"Are you sure?"
"I'm almost positive, every shapeshifter has a gland which aids in the ability to shape shift, and it also gives off a particular scent which only other shapeshifters can detect."
"So we're being watched?"
"It would appear so."
"But everyone has been here since the ceremony started so it couldn't be a person." I added.

Then a thought entered my head and I quickly looked back at the tree where I saw that large raven. The bird glanced down at me as if to let me know that it knew I was watching it. Its feathers and beak were so black that it melded almost perfectly with the night sky. It stared at me with a look of sheer anger and discuss as if I had done something terrible to it. Its eyes were as black as coal surrounded by a ring of bright yellow. As I continued to stare at the large bird, a wave of heat crashed into my body causing me to gasp once more. I took my eyes from the raven and concentrated on strengthening my aura but before I could summon up the extra energy, another more powerful wave of energy crashed into me. This time, it made me not only gasp for air but it knocked me backward sending me on the ground.

As I lay on my back looking up at Croix and Kiedan who were just about to help me back to my feet, I felt what I thought was a pin puncturing my skin. The sensation was not enough to make me cry out but it sure caught my attention.

There was another pinprick sensation and then another. Within moments, a shower of invisible pins rained down on me. Now the feeling of numerous invisible pins penetrating my skin caused me to cry out in pain.

Croix and Kiedan were now standing over me and attempted to shield me with their own auras from the invisible barrage of pins. Blood began to trickle from the many tiny holes now visible on my skin. I rocked from side to side in pain as the barrage of pins continued their assault. I started to feel like a living voodoo doll as the pins rained down into my very flesh. Croix and Kiedan could not see them but they could see the blood as it exited from every hole they made as they hit me. I could no longer control the volume of my screams and released a loud cry that attracted the attention of the others.

The crowd in front of us parted to either side, no longer had I noticed who exactly was surrounding me as I started to lose consciousness from the loss of blood. I felt my body slowly losing feeling and my mind felt as if I were intoxicated. Faint voices filled my ears but I was unable to make out what they were saying as I drifting into unconsciousness. Even the feeling from the continuous shower of invisible pins no longer affected me. I was heading into the void of darkness and silence where there was no substance. Was this to be my time to leave the physical word? All I could feel was air around me. I no longer had feeling in my limbs and there was no more pain either. All I could feel was the sensation of floating through nothingness. As I looked around into the darkness, I saw a light in the distance.

I began to float towards that light if nothing more than to simply satisfy my curiosity. I would not have known that I was actually moving through the darkness if not for the light before me growing bigger. The closer I came to it, the larger and brighter it became until I could no longer gaze upon it. It was then I realized exactly what was happening. The light I was looking upon was, in fact, the very same light, which encompassed the God and Goddess when I envisioned them earlier. "Lady and Lord was I actually dead?" Where they, in fact, coming to take me away? The light became soft and radiant and I could look upon it without flinching. Suddenly the mass of light broke into two separate orbs, which then started to take shapes of their own. I could see the formation of arms and legs on each but one started to form what would soon become firm ample breasts while the other formed a nice size manhood.

I could not believe my eyes when it was all said and done, I was once more standing in the presence of the Lady and Lord in all their magnificent glory. I was without words and even if I knew what to say, I do not think I could have even mustered up the courage to speak. The two brilliant shapes came closer towards me until they were just in breathing distance. Then ever so softly, they each laid a hand atop both of my shoulders. I looked at their shining bodies in amazement, their faces both held beautifully bright smiles. I suddenly felt like a helpless child standing in the presence of their greatness. It was then that the silence was interrupted by the softness of the Goddess's voice.

"Anora my dear child why did you allow yourself to be harmed in this manner?" She asked still holding that bright smile upon her lips.

"I don't know my Goddess it just came upon me."

"My child you are much stronger then you realize. This spell would not have harmed you this much if you knew your true potential."

"She is right my dear you are more powerful than you realize." Spoke the strong deep vibrating voice of the God.

"My dear mother and father of all Wicca I keep hearing that I'm supposed to be special but I don't feel it in any way."

"Oh but you are special my child." Said the Goddess as her hand moved from my shoulder and rested atop my own hand.

"I don't understand."

"You will soon enough my child but for now, you must return to the material plane for it is not your time to go to the Summerlands." Said the God whose voice seemed to shake every fiber of my being.

"I still don't quite understand my Lady and Lord but if you say that I am special then I believe you." I said in a soft low voice like that of a woman after giving birth.

"Do not trouble yourself my dear all will be revealed to you when time permits." Spoke the Goddess as she leaned in and embraced me.

"Your parents are most proud of you Anora." Spoke the God as the Goddess stepped back to allow him the opportunity to embrace me as well.

They stepped back from me and smiled once more. The smell of fresh flowers and a warm crisp summer breeze filled the air and all I could see was their luminescent bodies begin to grow more and more distant from my view. As their glow began to fade away, so too did the sweet scent of flowers. I started to hear voices in the distance but they did not belong to the Goddess and God. I felt something lifting my body upwards through the darkness, no longer did the bright bodies of the Goddess and God illuminated the sea of blackness and I was once more back where I started before their magnificent entry. As I continued to float upwards, I could hear the voices growing louder and more distinguishable. Then as if someone had taken a quick snapshot, I saw a brief flash of light that caused me to close my eyes. When I reopened them, I was laying in my bed surrounded by Aunt Ellice, Uncle Adler, Croix, Kiedan and Gretchen Wilkes.

It was light outside and the sun was passed its peak, which suggested that I was out for the duration of the night and the better half of the day. As I looked at those gathered around my bed, I could see that they all wore the same expression of shock and worry. However, it was the look on Croix's face, which caused me to hold my gaze on him the longest. His eyes were wide but I could tell that he was holding back tears, his lips twitched every so often, which was a dead giveaway that although he was worried, he was also happy to see me alive, and his hands were steadfast behind him which for him was yet another dead giveaway that he was nervous. I gave him a soft smile to assure him that I was fine and that I realized just how concerned he was.

He managed to stop the quivering of his lips just long enough to flash me a smile back, then he returned to his normal facial expression and his hands appeared from behind his back to rest on each side of his hips. Shortly after seeing the exchange of smiles between Croix and myself, I saw the faces of everyone else who was present begin to brighten as well. Clearly, they were relieved that I had not taken that step into the afterlife but was I really on the threshold between this plane and the spirit realm. Moreover, what does all of this talk about me being special truly mean? I must admit that I never took it seriously when Aunt Ellice would say it but now that it has come from the very lips of the Lady and Lord, how can I ignore it?

I started to zone out everyone around me while concentrating deeply on what transpired only moments ago when the sound of Aunt Ellice's voice and the touch of Croix's hand on my shoulder quickly brought me back to the reality at hand.

"Anora are you alright?" She spoke with a slight shakiness to her voice.
"Yes Aunt Ellice I'm fine but how long have I been asleep?"
"Asleep?" Bellowed Kiedan, "Anora you were far from asleep."
"What do you mean Kiedan if I wasn't asleep then what was I?"
"Try dead."

My eyes grew wide with fright and my lips parted to form an "oh" expression. I started to try to recall the events, which led to my supposed death.

Then I remembered the shower of invisible needles, how they pierced my skin, causing me to bleed. I remember being unable to shield myself from them and thus falling to the ground in an unconscious state but here I thought I had just passed out.

"You had us all worried you know?" Said Kiedan as he folded his arms across his chest.
"Well believe me I didn't mean to worry anyone. In fact, I had no idea I was even out for such a long time."
"Well, my dear I must admit that even I believed that you were destined for the Summerlands." Said Gretchen Wilkes who now had taken residence next to me on the bed, her hands placed gently on both sides of my face.

I was still weak from the whole ordeal but my curiosity demanded to be satisfied regardless of my weakened state. I wanted to know what happened during my alleged death and I would not allow myself to rest until I knew. I started to prop myself up in the bed as Kiedan and Croix assisted my efforts by placing the fluffy goose down pillows behind me as I leaned back against the bedpost.

"Tell me something, what happened after I lost consciousness?"

There was complete silence as I watched everyone in the room exchange glances as if silently asking who would be the one to tell the tale. I wondered exactly just how much I missed while unconscious or was it simply that they didn't know how to tell me what had happened in a way that would not upset me.

I remained calm and composed as I stared at them displaying nothing but complete patience on my face. After a few moments have elapsed, Croix finally spoke which was good, seeing that he was not one to sugarcoat. I knew if it came from him that it would be true and uncensored. Sparing my feelings was not an option right now.

"How much do you remember Anora?" He asked with a straight-faced look.

"Well, the last thing I remember is falling to the ground and being showered by large invisible needles."

"As you fell you let out such a scream that it made everyone at the initiation ritual turn to see what was going on. Although they couldn't see the needles, they saw your bloody body fall to the ground."

"Did they postpone the initiation ritual?"

"As a matter of fact, they did." This coming from Kiedan who now seemed comfortable enough to partake in the conversation.

"Really?" I could not help but be surprised that they had stopped for my sake.

"Yes they did, in fact, Gavin McLellan was very insistent on continuing the ritual." Replied Croix.

"Interesting, I wonder why the urgency?"

"After Kiedan and I brought you home, they eventually went ahead with the ceremony."

"Yes, in fact, it wasn't until we checked in on you afterward when we noticed that you were not with us as it were."

"Nice choice of words Croix." I said giving off just a hint of sarcasm in my voice.

"Well, I need to get out of this bed and start figuring out what's going on."

"Are you certain you're alright Anora?" Asked Aunt Ellice who remained silent throughout the entire conversation until now.

"I'm as alright as I can be Aunt Ellice thanks."

"Maybe we should have a doctor look at you first?"

"No need Aunt Ellice, besides I can almost guarantee you that a doctor would not find anything wrong."

"As you wish but please be careful, it's clear that someone wants you dead but why?" She wore the same look of confusion on her face as I when she said that for now, we were all wondering why.

I started to get out of bed when I noticed that all the men in the room quickly turned their backs to me. It was then I took the time and realized that underneath the soft cotton covers I was completely naked. By their sudden reaction, I could only assume that they had prior knowledge of this and were giving me the privacy I deserved. I could not help but let out a small chuckle since every man in attendance has seen me nude at one time or another. Nevertheless, it was nice to see that despite that fact, they still gave me the proper respect.

Gretchen Wilkes reached over and grabbed my silk robe from a nearby chair and I arose from the bed. I was still a bit woozy from my latest ordeal but I needed to get some answers and fast before something else happens. Kiedan and Croix assisted me to the closet and held me steady as I picked out something to wear. I was not thinking about making a fashion statement so I simply grabbed a pair of dark blue jeans and a purple V-neck shirt.

I knew I would be doing a lot of walking around or, at least, a good bit of standing so I reached inside my closet and brought forth a pair of black loafers to wear. I walked back to my bed and carefully laid the clothes out, then turning towards where I could have a good view of all the males in attendance I gave a waving gesture with my hands that it was time for them to take their leave. Sure, they have all seen me naked at one time or another, but even a free spirit such as myself deserves a moment of privacy from time to time. As the men slowly exited the room, I glanced at the faces of Aunt Ellice and Gretchen Wilkes who were smiling in that way young women do when it is time for girl talk. I needed a particular question answered and I knew that the answer could be found between either Aunt Ellice or Gretchen Wilkes.

"I have a question for you two." I began while removing my robe and slipping my one leg into the white silken panties that lay on the bed.

"Sure honey, what is it?" Asked Aunt Ellice still smiling.

"First, off I want to know exactly what really happened to my parents."

The two women's faces simultaneously changed from giddy smiles to serious frowns as neither one wanted to answer the question posed to them. While they exchanged glances, I continued to dress, sliding the silken panties up and then placing my bra over my breasts before fastening it. The two knew that I wasn't going to let them go without some sort of acknowledgment to my request and I think what they were doing was silently asking one another who would be the one to tell the tale surrounding my parents demise. I decided to help their decision along after noticing that I was almost completely dressed and they had not said a word.

"I don't expect an answer from you Gretchen but as for you Aunt Ellice, you are family so I should at least get some sort of explanation from you."

"I guess you deserve to know the truth now." Replied Aunt Ellice.

I was fully dressed now except for the shoes. I sat on the bed looking at the two women as they stood in front of me with their hands folded in front of their stomachs. Aunt Ellice sat beside me on the bed and Gretchen Wilkes pulled up a nearby chair and sat down. By the looks on their faces, I knew that I was in for quite a story therefore, I mentally prepared myself for whatever was to come.

"Well?" I asked fixing eyes first on Aunt Ellice then turning slightly to fix them on Gretchen Wilkes.

"To be honest Anora we don't really know what happened to your parents." This from Aunt Ellice who was now fidgeting with her fingers as she spoke, a clear sign that she was nervous.
"I don't understand. I was told they were murdered."

"Well they were but not by normal means."

"Then how were they murdered?"

"Their life forces were drained from them." Replied Gretchen Wilkes who was not going to let Aunt Ellice withstand the worst of this inquisition alone.

"How?" I asked.

"All we know is that shortly after your tenth birthday they were out in the fields together, the next thing we knew they were found dead, both naked and holding one another."

"Is this true Aunt Ellice?"

"Yes, child it is." She said lowering her head in sorrow.

I found myself deprived of words as I closed my eyes and began pondering what was just told to me. I wanted to yell at them, curse them for not conducting a more extensive investigation, but I could not to them at least. I opened my eyes and looked at them. In their eyes, I could see the pain and sorrow and that reinforced the decision not to persecute them.

I wanted to know what really happened to my parents but now was not the time. I had other things, dangerous things, which required my complete attention. Someone's out to deprive me of my life and I don't even have a clue as to who it is or why. All I know for sure is that whoever it may be, they must be the ones responsible for the theft of the Grand Grimoire, and they are most likely using the spells contained within the book to get me. I'm not a powerful witch but then again I'm also no armature either but how can I expect to combat against the magicks contained within the pages of the Grand Grimoire? We're talking about ancient and powerful magicks and if I don't do something soon to protect myself, I may not get to see my upcoming birthday.

Well, I surely wasn't going to get any answers here in my bedroom. I finished dressing and looked at the two women who have now risen from where they sat and began walking towards the door.

"What will you do now that you know the truth?" Asked Gretchen.

"Well I want to find who was responsible but I'm afraid that will have to wait."

"And what will you do about this current situation?"

"Until I get to the bottom of this I'll need some added protection." I said as I walked towards my altar. There, a small box sat. I opened it and took out a ring. The ring was made of pure silver with a carved Celtic knot design encircling the ring. This ring was blessed on a full moon and would provide me with a good dose of added protection for whatever awaited me in the moments ahead.

I placed the ring around my finger and with that I was ready to take on the day. I began walking towards the bedroom door and when I reached the threshold, both Aunt Ellice and Gretchen Wilks both escorted me downstairs and out to where the men were sitting anxiously awaiting. As we entered the living room, the men stood and watched us with gentleness in their eyes as they proved to be true men indeed, by acknowledging our presence.

"Glad to see you're feeling alright Anora." said Uncle Adler smiling.
"I'd feel a lot better once we get to the bottom of all this." I said as I walked over to the coffee table and picked up an apple from the fruit basket. As I bit into the dark reddish apple, I suddenly remembered the project which we were contracted to do for Gavin McLellan and I knew that I had yet one more thing to take care of.

"What time is it?" I asked.
"It's about twelve thirty-five why?" Inquired Uncle Adler
"I've got to get to work; I hope Bruce isn't upset with me when I get there."
"No worries hon, he called earlier and we told him you were ill so he said to come in only if you're up to it." Said Aunt Ellice.
"Well, that's one thing gone right so far thanks." I said taking yet another bite from the apple.
"Let me guess you're going to go to work aren't you?" Said Uncle Adler who didn't particularly like the idea that I was considering it.
"Yes, after all, I still have a responsibility to uphold and besides it will be a welcome distraction from all that has happened."
"Well don't think you're going into the city without me." Said Croix.
"I appreciate the gesture Croix but you're needed here."

"Nonsense, either I go or you stay."

"No sense arguing with him Anora, he's clearly made up his mind." Stated Aunt Ellice still wearing a smile on her face.

I looked at the faces of everyone in attendance and judging by their looks they were all in agreement with Croix's decision to accompany me into the city. Croix stood firm with his hands behind him and a stern look on his face. I knew he cared deeply for me and this was his chance to prove himself, so I smiled in acceptance, far be it for me to take away that which makes a man true.

"Alright, I guess it wouldn't hurt and you'll be in my office with me most of the time." I said as I took one final bite of the apple before disposing the remains into the wastebasket.

"Then it's settled, Croix will guard Anora while we search for answers." Said Gretchen Wilks.

I walked over to where Aunt Ellice and Uncle Adler stood and kissed them both goodbye. Then bestowing a gentle hug to Gretchen Wilks, I walked out of the living room and out the front door with Croix following closing behind. I had my personal power, the magick of the ring, and Croix with me now. Not that I would like to actually see it happen, but I thought to myself how I'd like to see someone attempt to magickally attack me now. Be careful what you wish for, even if you didn't mean to wish it.

Chapter Seven

The air was crisp and warm as I stepped outside. There was a strong breeze which when it struck me, caused my hair to fly outwards like the spreading wings of some gigantic bird. The glow of the sun made me squint for a moment as I wasn't quite over the darkness of my bedroom. After I finally adjusted to the brightness of the day, I looked around at the scenery. The leaves were beginning to lose their green color and were transforming into the hard brownish texture which usually comes with the changing of the season. I walked towards my car with Croix still closely behind me. He was dressed in black jeans with a matching black shirt and black boots. We arrived at the car and got in when Croix looked at me with that serious "I wish you'd reconsider" look on his face.

"Is there something you want to say Croix?" I asked as I fastened my seatbelt and started the car.

"Yes but perhaps it's not my place to comment." He said as he fastened his seat belt. I knew he wanted to say what was on his mind but being the man that he is, he would not say it if it would disrespect me in some way.

"Go on Croix, say what's on your mind."

I put the car in drive and stepped on the gas. We pulled out of the driveway and down the road. I felt Croix's stare as we drove towards the main highway. He was concentrating on exactly how to word what he wanted to say without emotionally hurting me. The thought of this made me smile slightly which was a welcomed treat given the recent circumstances.

I realized that we were midway down the highway and getting ever so close to the city. If he wanted to tell me something, he had better do it quickly before we reached our destination. I figured that if I don't say something to coax him into speaking he'll sit there forever fighting for the right words.

"Croix just come out and say it and stop worrying about sparing my feelings."

" Fine, I think you're making a big mistake in going to work." He said feeling somewhat relieved that he no longer had to trip over his words.

"Well, your concerns have been duly noted but isn't that why you're here?"

"Yes but I still feel that you should have remained home where it was safest."

"Croix in case you haven't noticed, there's not many places where I can feel safe right now." I stated as I turned off the highway and onto the main street leading downtown.

"Exactly why you should have stayed home where there are more people who can protect you from whatever or whomever is doing this to you."

I couldn't help but hear the caring in his voice. I've never thought of Croix as the type of man who would easily show emotions not to mention such sensitive ones as caring or even love. Croix was a hard man, a man of honor and values. In a world where chivalry is all but dead, Croix could have been considered one of the last of the true gentlemen of the cause. Although I did like that fact about him, it also at times proved to be quite annoying like right now.

"Croix I can't explain the previous happenings but the last two incidents have one thing in common." I stated as we pulled up to the street where the building which housed my place of employment stood.

"Oh, and what would that be?" He asked with a slightly puzzled look on his face.

"I just realized that in the last two incidents Gavin McLellan was present."

I could tell he was thinking about that for a moment then with widened eyes he looked at me, grabbed my free arm, and leaned slightly closer to me. He was about to say something which by the look in his eyes was about to probably cause me to have an accident.

"Oh shit Anora I just remembered something."

"Do tell Croix." I said as we slowed down to turn into the underground parking lot of the office building.

"You began having these attacks three days ago correct?"

"Yes."

"Well the night prior to your first incident in your bedroom Gavin came to the community to speak with the council members regarding his initiation into the coven."

"Let me guess he stayed overnight?"

"Correct, he stayed in the inn because it was too late to leave after he'd talked with them."

I was right. If not for the fact that we had already pulled into a parking spot I surely would have had an accident after hearing that. I took my arm from his grip and placed both hands on the steering wheel. I closed my eyes while holding a death grip on the wheel. The shock and horror were sufficient grounds for my reaction.

"And the incident in the conference room that day." I said still holding firmly onto the steering wheel.

"When we were first introduced to Gavin?" Asked Croix.

"Yes, I had this sudden rush of energy through the lower region of my body." I replied.

"Sex magick." He said.

"What?"

"He was using sex magick on you I would assume with the hopes that you'd respond."

I started to feel a heavy load in the pit of my stomach and my throat became as dry as the hottest desert. Could all of this be true and if so why? Why was he so interested in me to go as far as to use magick on me? I wanted to get to the bottom of all this but then again I also was afraid of what could happen if I did. Croix knew what I was thinking just by the look on my face. He knew I wasn't too happy with what I had just realized about my employer's newest client but right now, the best thing for me to do is to pretend as if I had no knowledge and keep a close eye on our friend.

"I can see you're not happy Anora." He said as he removed his seat belt and opened the passenger side door.

"Am I that transparent?" I replied as I also removed my seatbelt and stepped out of the car.

"Indeed and I don't blame you for being frightened."

"Frightened hardly, pissed off is more like it though I am a bit concerned."

"You're wondering if he's the cause of everything that's been happening to you."

"Yes but the big question is why?"

We walked towards the elevators and pressed the up button. The air in the underground garage was warm and stiff like the humidity in Midsummer. I closed my eyes and concentrated on my aura. I wanted all my defenses strengthened before I came in contact with Gavin McLellan again. The elevator door opened and we stepped in.

"So why don't we just get him alone and question him about it?"

"Because right now all we have is coincidence and speculation; we don't have any hard proof that he's responsible." I said as the elevator began its ascent.

"That's true and the only way that we can get proof is to catch him in the act but that will put you at risk again."

The elevator stopped and the doors opened. The brightness of the hall caused me to squint for a moment as we walked down the hall and into the double glass doors were the receptionist area was. I noticed that Alicia wasn't at the front desk so I took the liberty and signed our names to the sign-in sheet. We walked down the hallway and into my office. Sometimes I wonder if Bruce has a six sense when it comes to knowing when I'm in my office because once again, no sooner did I sit down and attempt to turn on my computer to check my email, he walked in. He was casually dressed which was normal for a Friday.

"Well hello, Anora glad you could make it in today." He said smiling.

"Thank you, Bruce, I'm sorry if I worried you."

"Well I have to admit when your Aunt mentioned that you were ill I was a tad concerned but I'm pleased that it wasn't as bad as I had originally thought."

I stared at him and thought to myself how interesting it would be if I could tell him why I was in bed just to see his reaction but I knew that I couldn't for quite a few obvious reasons, one of which being that if he knew he'd be in danger of being attacked just for knowing. Sounds nuts I know but even in the Craft when one works dark magicks they, like murders, tend to not leave any witnesses. This was one of those cases where ignorance was not only bliss but a life saver.

"So are you ready?" He asked as he held up a binder labeled McLellan.
"I'm as ready as I'm going to be." "Given the circumstances." I thought to myself.
"Oh and good day to you Croix." He added.
"Good day Bruce."

Croix walked over and offered Bruce his hand. The two men exchanged looks as if they were discussing something with their facial expressions then they gripped hands and shook. Of course, nothing could have prepared me for what came out of Bruce's mouth next as if he knew he could ask this of the man in front of him without incident.

"So tell me are you and Anora involved?"
"Um well no not really." He said with a slight smile which seemed to border along the lines of embarrassment.
"Forgive me for asking but our dear Anora isn't one for volunteering information especially when it pertains to her."
"Uh hello I am still in the room boys just in case you might have forgotten." I said as I stared up from my monitor at the two men who were still facing one another both sporting smiles.
"Sorry, Anora but it's just harmless guy talk." Stated Bruce as he looked at Croix for some sign of support for that statement. He didn't have to wait long for judging by the now larger grin on Croix's face, he did approve of the statement.

Outnumbered in my own office no less. I just couldn't catch a break lately. I stood up from my desk and walked towards the door passing the two men on my way without so much as a glance in their direction. I'm sure they must have thought I was upset but honestly I was just tired of the amount of testosterone being released in the air.

I walked down the hallway to the employee lounge area. I would soon realize that I really shouldn't have done that without Croix. Sitting inside near one of the huge windows was Gavin McLellan and Silvia who was standing right by his side. I was beginning to wonder if he ever allowed her to sit or did she prefer to stand. I couldn't turn back now so I entered in. The air felt thick and cool but heavy on the lungs when breathed in. Silvia fixed angry eyes on me once more. I guess it was safe to assume that she just did not like me for some reason or another but her stare had enough substance that it brushed across my body like an invisible wall.

Gavin, on the other hand, stood up and flashed that perfect smile at me with wide eyes. This made Silvia even angrier as she turned briefly towards him and then back to me with rage in her expression. If looks could kill, I'd be dead twenty times over by now but come to mention it there are some spells where just a look can do harm so with that fact in mind, I began to reinforce my aura. Although I wasn't completely clear as to Gavin McLellan's intentions towards me, Silvia wasn't as discreet. She wanted me gone in a big way. I searched her face trying to figure out what she was thinking other than the obvious which was to have me dead and buried somewhere far from her precious Gavin. I knew she didn't like me much but why? I guess I'll find out one way or another.

"My dear Anora how wonderful it is to see you again." Said Gavin as he stood up in front of his chair. He was all smiles complete with that twinkle in his eye. He had all the charm of a person who just killed his loved one and was out to make the world believe that he was innocent. Silvia, on the other hand, wasn't quick to hide how she felt towards me.

Just then, Bruce and Croix entered the lounge and came to stand next to me, thank you Lady and Lord. Gavin was now facing Bruce and myself, Silvia inched herself behind him so that she could show me how discussed she was without interruption from her employer. Silvia had the look of a black widow about to kill her prey in her eyes, and she was directing that gaze towards yours truly.

She wasn't going to take her eyes off of me as long as I remained in the same room as her boss, but I was beginning to suspect that she was suffering from a severe case of the green-eyed monster. I don't know why she'd think that I was interested in Gavin McLellan, and then it hit me like the impact from a one hundred mile an hour fastball. She despised me because her boss was infatuated with me, and he wasn't shy about displaying it either.

Gavin started to walk towards us still wearing that killer smile while Silvia remained where she stood. There was a feeling of a shift in the air as if there were a jet stream in the room. Somehow, Gavin was manipulating the very air in the room, at that point, my heart stopped as I suddenly put the two pieces together. Gavin McLellan was the one who used air magick on me in the bedroom that morning. Croix's suspicions were correct there was no mistaking that fact that Gavin was the one who has been attacking me. Well, I now know the who, now I need to know the why?

Well, one thing was certain, I wasn't going to just stand here and let that jealous bitch intimate me. Before I knew it, Gavin was now standing in front of Bruce and myself, still smiling of course, but I was now aware of his intentions towards me at least. I concentrated on my aura and envisioned it as a strong bright shield surrounding my body. I guess my efforts were successful because Gavin took a few steps backward and the smile faded. I could tell that Gavin was now searching for words in light of what he was currently feeling from my charged aura. Silvia also felt the energy but that only fueled her anger even more. I didn't think Gavin was the type to cave so quickly and sure enough, I was right. That slick bastard recovered faster than a man on Viagra and that smile was back in full bloom.

"And Mr. Kirkpatrick good day to you." He said.
"Good day to you to Mr. McLellan." I said, giving him a smile which pissed off Silvia even more.
"I've seen some of the works by your colleagues and they look fabulous, I can't' wait to see your contribution."
"I'm sure you'll be very satisfied." Replied Bruce as he glanced at me with a grin.
"Oh so far my good man, I can't help but agree with you."

"Would you two gentlemen excuse me I have to use the women's bathroom." I said. I didn't really have to go, I just wanted to get away from Gavin. It seemed that increasing my auric shield has only succeeded in making him more attracted to me.

I took my leave of the two men and went down the hall towards the woman's restroom. I entered the brightly lit room and stood in front of the full-length mirror on the wall. I took in a deep breath to settle my nerves, when I heard the sound of a woman's heels entering the room but I paid little attention to them. It wasn't until I saw Silvia behind me that I quickly turned to look.

"Finally bitch, it's just you and me."

I turned around to find Silvia's eyes fixed on me like that of a predator about to pounce. Her hands were balled into fists and resting on her hips. This wasn't going to be good nor easy for me. I was casually dressed which meant that if this were to erupt into a cat fight I wouldn't have to worry about losing much in the way of clothing as I would have had I've been wearing a dress or skirt. Silvia stood there in her black dress pants and black silk top, her hair was pulled back in the same ponytail she wore when we first met. I thought to myself that this wasn't going to end the way I'd like it to but I should, at least, try to reason with the woman in the hopes that perhaps she'd listen. I blinked at the woman then stood in a casual pose trying not to show any signs of a willingness to fight with her.

"Silvia I know what you must be thinking but I assure you it's not the way in which you perceive it." I said in a calm neutral tone.
"Is that so? And what am I thinking?"
"You think that I am inviting the advances of your boss Gavin McLellan and I assure you that couldn't be far from the truth." I replied still managing to keep my tone at a normal level.
"You sure are a conceded little bitch aren't you?" She said as she took a step forward. I could see then that this wasn't going to be easy and that she had already made up her mind that she wanted a piece of me. Lady and Lord help me, if I knew I'd have to go through this I would have stayed home after all.

"Silvia isn't it? Look I don't want any trouble."

"Then you should have remained dead the first time we crossed paths." She said with a slight snarl to her voice.

"The first time?" I asked since the first time I recall meeting her was in the conference room.

"I honestly don't know what the master sees in you but you're not taking his favor away from me."

By now, she was ready for a fight. She took a step back and started to raise her right hand. Without thinking, I rose my left hand and concentrated my auric energy to my palm. The next thing I knew, there were two large orbs of energy flying from our hands, a loud boom could be heard as they collided in the middle of the room, and we were both flying backward against opposite walls of the bathroom. I wasn't sure what just happened, all I knew was that I had concentrated on projecting my auric energy outwards from my palm in the hopes that it would push Silvia backward enough for me to run but instead it seems she had the same idea and the force of both our auras sent us both backward. This truly wasn't going to end peacefully after all.

We both stood up slowly as pieces of tile fell from the walls. Silvia rose to her feet with a look of surprise on her face. She wasn't the only one who was surprised but I didn't let my face show it. I could always move small objects with my thoughts and with auric energy but I never did something as heavy as what just happened. I only wanted to push her back and instead, I ended up sending her flying back into a wall. Now wasn't the time to figure this out I still have to get through this ordeal with Silvia who had now changed her look from surprise to sheer fury.

"You little Wiccan bitch." She said. She had that look in her eyes that she would not be happy until she placed me underground and lifeless, but I wasn't ready to visit the afterlife again so I began concentrating on strengthening my aura once more.

I envision myself surrounded by a triple bluish-white light. Silvia raised both her hands to her chest and crossed them, then in one motion she flung them outward and I felt an invisible force slam against my aura like a train slamming into a wall. The shock drew me back a few steps but not as far as it should have.

I couldn't help but wonder what else happened to me while I was unconscious, or was I receiving some much-needed help from other forces? I looked at Silvia who was getting ready to strike at me again but this time, I wasn't going to allow her the first blow.

I concentrated hard on my energy and closed my eyes for a moment. I envisioned my body vibrating with energy and my aura shining as bright as the moon itself. Silvia must have sensed what I was doing and immediately began strengthening her own auric energy. The air grew warm with the heat from our bodies. I noticed the whites of Silvia's eyes begin to shine brighter until her pupils disappeared.   I lost all sense of fear and the most basic of survival instincts took hold of me.   I balled my hands into fists and focused all my energy on them. Silvia had once more crossed her arms over her chest and balled her hands into fists. There we both stood poised for battle as if we were a part of a Mexican standoff, each person awaiting the others move.

The walls started to shake from the vibrations of our auras, Silvia started to unfurl her hands which was my queue to make my move. Once more we both ended up discharging our energies at the same time at one another but this time, the energies were so intense that when they collided the shock not only sent both of us backward again, but the combine blast of psychic energies destroyed the bathroom almost completely. The sinks and toilets shattered like rock candy. The mirrors shattered as well into hundreds of pieces and the tiles on the walls burst from the foundation. The sound of the blast caught the attention of the others who were still in the conference room. As I rose to my feet slightly staggering in the process, I heard banging at the door.

Silvia shook her head and also started to stand as the banging continued. I heard Croix and Bruce outside asking if we were alright. I was out of breath from the force of the blast and could not gather enough wind to speak. Silvia appeared to be unable to speak as well while looking at me with that surprised face again. Suddenly the door flew open and bodies poured in. Croix and Bruce ran over to me as Gavin McLellan tended to Silvia. I felt water falling from my head and into my face, it was then when I looked around and noticed that water was shooting out from where the sinks and toilets once were.

Even the tile on the walls fell victim to the force of the blast. Tiny bits of tile and shattered glass littered the floor. I looked around the room to see who had come in when I suddenly became dizzy and fell to the floor on my hands and knees. Croix and Bruce each took an arm and brought me back to my feet. I looked over to where Silvia and Gavin McLellan were standing. Silvia looked a little disoriented but the look on Gavin's face made me wonder. He stared at me as he held up his assistant with a look of admiration and border-lined lust in his eyes. He apparently was excited to see what had happened here. Murray, Craig, Delia, and Alicia were now standing at the door all showing the same horrific expressions.

"What in the hell happened?" Asked Murray who spoke for the others as well as himself.
"Not now Murray, go tell maintenance to shut off the water up here." Said Bruce as he continued to help hold me up.

Murray turned and walked away while the others remained at the door still looking in at all of the damage. There were about four inches of water on the floor now and if the valves weren't shut off soon, it would start to leak to the floors below.

"I suggest we get everyone out of here." Said Croix who by now probably realized what truly had happened and therefore, sought to put some distance between Silvia and me.

The two men proceeded to escort me past Gavin McLellan and his assistant who was now beginning to regain her composure as she once more fixed angry eyes at me.

As I passed the two, Silvia suddenly grabbed hold of my arm and drew herself close enough that her lips were touching my ear.

"This isn't over bitch mark my words, I will have my retribution." She whispered and the heat from her breath was more than enough to send shivers down my back, but I did my best not to show her just how intimidating her words were to me. I drew back enough so that I could look her in the face.

"For your sake, I hope there won't be a next time." I whispered and with that I walked out of the ruined bathroom with my male escorts hoping that this was the last encounter I would have with Silvia but for some reason, I kind of doubted it.

Chapter Eight

I was soaked through, even my panties were drenched. I went into my office, still escorted by Croix and Bruce. I needed a change of clothes and a towel but right now, I was happy to be alive. Silvia was clearly playing for keeps back there and I'm certain that she won't hesitate should we meet again one on one and yet all this did nothing more than put another question in my head. What makes her believe that I'm competition for her? But even more important is how in the hell did I manage to do what I did back there? Oh sure I have some abilities, but I couldn't do anything like what I just did in that bathroom let alone at that magnitude.

Croix released my arm once we entered the room and stood next to the window, Bruce who was still clutching my other arm had a look of wonderment and surprise to his face. I didn't have to be a rocket scientist to figure out that he was highly curious as to how the women's bathroom got to look as it did. Croix, on the other hand, didn't look as surprised. In fact, he had a slight hint of a grin on his face as he looked at me one moment and out the window the next.

Alicia came to the door, she still held that surprised look as well but she did not comment on any of the events leading to the destruction of the women's bathroom. She seemed more interested in getting Bruce's attention.

"Uh, Mr. Kirkpatrick the maintenance men wish to speak to you regarding the state of the women's bathroom."

Bruce let go of my arm and walked towards the opened door where Alicia stood. He turned around once more and glanced at me.

"Any ideas as to what I should tell them Anora?" He asked with a slight chuckle.

I looked at Croix who was still standing near the window swapping glances between the view and me. I started drying my hair using those rough but very absorbent hand towels that most businesses use in their restrooms. It wasn't until I began drying my hair when I happened to look down and noticed that my breasts were making an appearance through my top. I was soaked and therefore, eligible to enter a wet t-shirt contest. Surprisingly, neither man in the room commented. I guess they figured that if they had, I would have found some way to cover up and therefore, spoil their view. Men will be men I suppose, so let them look, after all, I owed them for their timely rescue.

"You could always tell them the truth Bruce."
"And what would the truth be?"
"That there was an explosion."

Bruce looked at me with that surprised gaze as if to say "Are you serious?" I continued drying my hair and attempted to ring out the excess water from my clothes, keeping in mind that my breasts were still superimposed underneath my top. My nipples were erect and protruding outwards, after all, the water was cold. Bruce shook his head in confusion and walked out the door with Alicia trailing behind. No sooner had he disappear from view, Croix turned wide eyes towards me, a slight grin was visible on his face.

"Care to share?" He said as he walked towards me.
"She wanted me dead it seems."
"Well that part was obvious but what I want to know is where did that power come from?"
"Honestly Croix I don't know, all I know is that I wanted to just push her back out of the way so I could escape and well the rest is history."
"Well I know this much I'll be careful not to piss you off from now on." He said smiling.

I closed my eyes and smiled back, thinking all the while "Great another riddle to solve." Lady and Lord help me can't I at least get the answers to the ones I already have first?

I stood in front of my desk in my wet clothes thinking how I needed to get dry before I became sick, not to mention, the peep show I was unwillingly giving.

"I need dry clothes." I said as I once more rang the excess water from my attire. But I had to wonder exactly what excuse did Bruce give the maintenance guys and did they believe him?

"You know your Aunt and Uncle will want to hear of this incident?"

"Yes and I think it best if it came from your lips instead of mine."

"And why is that?" He asked with that slightly confused look on his face.

"Because you don't know the details and if you don't know them, neither will they."

"And what if I wish to know the details for myself?" He replied. The confused look had disappeared and in its place was that serious expression he would display when he was trying not to release his anger.

I knew that if I were to tell him the complete story he'd keep it a secret if I asked him but at this point in time, I didn't want to go back to that moment as it was still burning fresh in my mind. Every horrific moment flashing past my eyes every time I blinked. All I wanted to do now was change my clothes and move onward with my life.

I walked over to where he stood and placed my hand against his cheek. His face although frozen with seriousness was warm and soft to the touch. I started to caress his face with my hand giving gentle strokes up and down his cheek. The feeling made his eyes close and soon after, the serious face disappeared and in its place was that soft gentle Croix which excited me so much.

I stopped the caress and leaned into him. I parted my lips and kissed him softly, closing my eyes and thinking of nothing but that moment. Croix's arms reached around my waist and pulled me closer to him. He began to respond to my kiss by pressing his lips into mine.

I could no longer feel the dampness of my clothes as we embraced but instead I felt only the warmth of my own body as it tingled with tiny sensations. We soon forgot that we were in my office as we continued kissing and caressing one another. Croix's hands found their way underneath my shirt and had begun stroking my back ever so slowly that I could feel the trails of heat as he did. The feeling made me breathe deeply and I pressed even harder into the kiss now giving him a little tongue on top of it.

Although they were closed, I could feel the burning sensation of the whites of my eyes as they filled with auric energy, the pulsing of energies between Croix and I caused my aura to ignite like gasoline when lit. Croix's aura was also growing as he probed my throat with his tongue. I wanted to forget the incidents which happened, I wanted to forget about that evil, she bitch Silvia and that obsessed employer of hers Gavin McLellan. I wanted to forget having to find out who stole the Grand Grimoire or even how my parents died.

All I wanted to remember was this kiss and how it was making me feel right now. I wanted to be taken, to be ravaged as only Croix could do it. To feel his hands all over my body, exploring every inch of me. But most of all, I wanted him inside me, to feel every inch of him that I could manage in me. He must have been reading my thoughts for he had ceased caressing my bare back and placed his hands on my buttocks, gripping them as one would grip a ball. This caused me to press tight against him.

We suddenly drew back from the kiss and looked at one another. Croix's eyes grew wide as he searched my face to find the hidden meaning of its expression. It didn't take him long to figure it out, he drew me close to him once more, pulled my hair back to expose my ear, and pressed his lips to it.

"Anora much as I'd like to accommodate your wish, I think it's time that we excused ourselves from here and head back home if nothing more than to get you some dry clothes."
"I guess you're right." I said with a deep sigh.

"But don't think that I won't forget this moment as I shall be patiently awaiting the right time to continue where we left off." He replied.

"I don't doubt it Croix." I said with a smile.

I grabbed my things and headed out of the office with Croix close behind. We reached the lobby where Bruce was standing next to the receptionist desk. He had that confident male ego look on his face which suggested that he somehow explained to the maintenance men the reason for the damage to the women's bathroom. I could tell by the smirk on his face that he couldn't wait to spill the beans on how he managed it. Far be it for me to ruin a man's ego especially when that man had a hand in saving my life. I was still damp from head to toe but I've been in these wet clothes all this time, I guess I could suffer for a few moments more. I walked up to Bruce and placed a hand on his face.

"I'm sorry for putting the responsibility of explaining things on you like that Bruce."

"Oh well I admit it was challenging but I'd do anything for you." He said.

"And for that, I thank you." I said slightly turning red in the face from his comment. Bruce was a man of his word so if he said he'd do anything for me, I could rest assure that he meant it.

"So tell me, what exactly did you tell them?"

He loosened his tie just enough for his Adam's apple to show then he leaned on the edge of the receptionist desk striking a pose that you'd find in a men's catalog.

"I simply told them that several pipes had burst. After all, there was enough water on the floor to substantiate it."

"Bruce you're a true genius." I said as I gave him a damp hug. I was so happy that the matter wasn't going to continue thanks to his quick-thinking that I had forgotten that I was still damp from the water until I pressed my body against his. Needless to say he didn't mind the dampness of the embrace as he wrapped his arms around me and held me close to him.

Bruce would endure just about anything if it meant the chance of holding me close to him even for a brief moment. I leaned back from the embrace to notice the water markings that I had made on his nicely pressed suit. I started to feel bad that I had caused it until I happened to notice the huge grin on his face. He was happy that I had embraced him and the smile on his face reassured me that no matter what damage I may have caused to his suit, all was forgiven. I turned my attention to Croix who was sporting an equally large smile. I wanted to know what he was all smiles about but didn't want to say it aloud so I closed my eyes and concentrated on him, then in my mind I started to speak.

"And what are you all smiles about mister?"
"I can't help but notice how with just a mere embrace, you made that man's day." He said.
"Yeah well I'm glad that you enjoyed it."
"Oh very much so however, I can't help but wonder."
"Wonder what?"
"If he gets that happy over a hug, how would he react if you fucked him?"
"Well, I'm not ready to find that out." I stated as I opened my eyes thus breaking my concentration and ending our conversation.

When I opened my eyes and turned back to look at Bruce again, his smile had turned into a small grin as he stared at the two of us. He was wondering what was transpiring between Croix and I or perhaps he was just feeling like a third wheel at this point.

"You know I'll never get used to you doing that." He said with a slight chuckle in his voice.
"Used to what Bruce?" I asked attempting to play coy.
"That whole telepathy thing that you do."
"I'm sorry Bruce, it's rude for us to do that in the company of others who can't participate." I said.

Croix looked at us with that stiff stone-cold face. I've always known about his little pet peeve when it comes to that fact that those with gifts have to cater to those without them.

I'll never forget his reaction when Congress passed a law which prohibited advanced psychics from reading people's thoughts without their consent. I guess one can't help but feel the same way if the roles were somehow reversed. Even though everyone born of this Earth possesses psychic abilities, but not everyone is able or willing to undergo the processes necessary to achieve this. However, they demand some sort of protection against those who have reached such levels of psychic awareness. Bruce is not only my boss but a good friend and for that, he deserves some respect.

I looked into the eyes of the man who was still holding me and smiled at him. I could tell he knew that the purpose for the smile was to acknowledge that I respected him and apologized for not adhering to the laws governing psychic usage in the city.

"I'm sorry Bruce it won't happen again I promise."
"No worries, it just gives me a reason to practice more." He said smiling.
"We really ought to be going Anora." Stated Croix, as he checked the time on his wristwatch. He clearly wanted to get out of the city to the more familiar ground and for once, I didn't blame him.

I took a small step back from Bruce's embrace and placed my hand on his cheek to signify how grateful I was for the nice cover-up job he recently performed on my behalf. I made a mental note to properly thank him when all of this was over but for now, I needed to get home, into some dry clothes, and figure out what to do next. I gave my boss, good friend, and lifesaver one final hug before turning towards the elevator door.

"Anora wait!" Cried Bruce.

I turned around to give the man one more look at my figure which was showing underneath the dampness of my clothes.

"Yes, Bruce."
"If I can help in any way, don't hesitate to call me you hear?" He said smiling.

"Thank you, Bruce, but given the depth of the situation, I dare not risk your life like that."

"Hey, I wouldn't have offered if I wasn't prepared to accept the consequences."

I walked back over to where he stood and stopped directly in front of him. Staring into his eyes, I cupped his face in my hands and stood up on my tiptoes to align his lips to mine. With one gesture, I kissed the man who has proven himself to be more than just my employer, but a good and loyal associate. It was for this reason why I couldn't allow any harm to befall him.

I stepped back away from him when I felt his hand grip my arm. I looked briefly at his hand then at the man himself in the hopes to read his motives upon his face. His eyes were wide, his pupils glistened with tears. His mouth tightly closed as if he were desperately attempting to hold back any signs of emotional collapse.

For years I knew this man to be a strong individual and yet now in this moment, I could see that behind that tough exterior, was a vulnerable person wanting to reach out and share his feelings with me but with the fear of losing the perception I had of him.

"Now you're not going to go and loose it on me are you?" I asked while cracking a smile.

"Are you making light of the situation and for my benefit?" He replied still holding back the emotions as best as he could.

"Yes Bruce I am because I can see that you care."

"Well you've become more than just a mere employee to me."

"And I appreciate that dearly but I can't involve you in this." I said.

"But it appears you're going to need all the help you can get." He replied touching the side of my face with his hand.

"Like I said, I can't afford to have something happen to you."

"Are you suggesting that I can't hack it?"

Now he began to get upset as if I had just attacked his manhood or something. At this point, I didn't know how to exactly convey to him just how dangerous this undertaking would be.

I may be mortal like him, but I am realizing that I have been touched by the Lady and Lord in ways he could only imagine. Therefore, I am protected to some degree but he is truly mortal in every sense of the word and would not last long in a battle of mind and magicks.

"Bruce please don't pursue this I beg you." I pleaded as I placed both hands upon his shoulders.

Croix started walking towards us with that serious look on his face. He had his shoulders raised and his chest out as he approached. The sight of this made Bruce stare at the man waiting to see what was to become of this apparent confrontation. Croix stopped just inches of us and looked directly into the eyes of Bruce.

"Mr. Kirkpatrick I think that given the circumstances you reframe from taking any unnecessary actions in regards to this situation." He said with that stern voice of his.
"So you feel that I can't cut it either do you?"
"Yes sir I do, in fact, I'm not certain that any of us involved can."
"Then you agree that you can use all the help you can get right?"
"I do but not if it means certain death for the one who's helping."

The two men paused and stared at one another, each firmly standing his ground. This conversation was taking way too much time and I really wanted if nothing more, was to get into some dry clothes. Bruce opened his mouth as if to begin speaking when Croix interrupted him abruptly.

"Mr. Kirkpatrick you would do Anora a better service if she knew that you were not in harm's way."

Bruce stared at Croix noticing that the man was wearing a face which showed complete and utter seriousness. He then turned back towards me, eyes now closed and head slightly lowered. At that moment I could see that he was hurting inside but Croix was right.

I wouldn't be able to concentrate on the tasks at hand if I knew he'd be in harm's way, nor could I forgive myself should anything happen to him as a result of assisting me, even though I could sure use all the help I could get. I stood there silently waiting for the right moment to say something but finding that it wasn't coming anytime soon. Bruce parted his eyelids just enough to see, his eyes were glossy from the tears which he was struggling to hold back. He took my hands into his and drew in a deep breath. I knew that whatever he was going to say next wouldn't be easy for him so I made a conscious decision not to argue or respond, but instead to just simply listen.

"Promise me that you'll at least be careful and call me if you need to?" He said still holding my hands in his.

What could I say to him? Here's a man who has been a good boss and willing participant in my personal friend zone and yet, I couldn't bring myself to tell him what I really thought. How can I look into his tearful eyes and tell him that there's the possibility that I may not come to work one day in the near future due to a death in the family, my death in particular? I quickly scrambled through the mound of random thoughts which floated inside my head for the one best suited for this situation. Sometimes it's beneficial to think before speaking especially when the feelings of others are involved. I finally found the one best suited but not quite my first choice but hell, beggars can't be choosers.

"I promise that if I need you, I'll contact you." I said in my most reassuring voice.
"Well take as much time as you need and don't worry about the McLellan account, I'll put Murray on it."

His voice was shaky which meant that he really wasn't happy with his decision but under the circumstances, he had no other recourse. I stared into his eyes, trying to offer some hint of reassurance to the promise which I had just made, but I knew I'd failed.

Bruce was a straight shooter and wanted the same in return so I merely nodded my head in agreement, and gripped his hands. Croix was now becoming impatient from waiting as he wasn't one for waiting in the first place, let alone for extended amounts of time, so it came as no surprise that he was getting agitated by now.

"I hate to break up this party but we really ought to be going." He said using his calm yet serious voice.

"He's right." Bruce noted thus agreeing with Croix. "It's not safe here for you right now so go and be safe."

I gave Bruce one last hug making a point to push my breasts into his chest. After all, if I'm to die from all this, might as well give him something good to remember me by. The firmness of his chest and the overall warmth of his body gave me, if nothing more than a brief feeling of security and safety even though I knew it would be short-lived. As I stepped back to get a full look at him, I remembered my first day of employment, sitting on the other side of his large maple desk silent while he reviewed my credentials. That was a little over three years ago and here we are now standing here as more than just employee and employer but as friends.

I walked over towards the glass doors leading to the elevators, all the while wondering what will happen next. Croix kept a steady pace next to me making certain that his large steps didn't cause me to trail too far behind him. We entered the elevators completely silent, neither one wanted to be the ice-breaker but both itching to converse. As the large metallic cube slid down the shaft to the parking level, I thought to myself of all the events which have transpired up to this point. I turned to look at the tall handsome man next to me, although I'd never admit it to him for fearing that his already over confident male ego would grow to wondrous proportions.

How could I ask him or anyone else to just risk their lives for the sake of my own? Especially when I don't even know what's in store. As the elevator reached the parking level, and the doors slowly creaked open with that strange mechanical creaking sound, I took in a deep breath and began to walk towards the car. Croix had already reached the vehicle and had opened the passenger side door for me.

I stopped in front of him and placed a hand upon his cheek, not caring if my facial expression had given away my true feelings for no matter what, I did want him to realize that if nothing more, I do care a great deal for him and for all that he's done for me thus far.

Croix flashed his "Harlequin Romance" smile as he took my hand from his face and held it tight as if to reassure me that not only would he always be there for me but that in the end, everything would be alright. As I stepped into the car and began to secure myself with the seat belt, I couldn't help but ask myself, "If the end would be alright, what about the parts in-between?" Croix hopped into the driver's seat and with one motion, and no hands, he started the car and fastened his seat belt. I looked at him and smiled childishly. It's not every day when we get to have fun with our powers. He gave me a boyish grin and then stuck in the ignition key for appearance sake.

"So what are you going to do for an encore, drive with no hands?"
"Now there's a thought but we don't want to attract any attention now do we?"

Somehow that one brief conversation gave me a slight feeling of happiness and joy, from times once lived and hopefully of good ones to come. We drove down the highway laughing like kids all the way home. It was certainly a much well-needed distraction.

Chapter Nine

In a large condo overlooking the outskirts of the city, Silvia paced about, her fists clenched at her waist. She was not at all pleased with the recent events particularly the one which took place between she and I in the women's restroom at my place of employment. Over in a nearby brown leather reclining chair sat Gavin McLellan, his fingers interlaced together in a prayer-like manner with his chin resting atop them. Although he too was not entirely pleased, his thoughts were on what he considered to be of more importance than a mere magickal cat fight. Silvia stopped in the middle of the room and slammed her foot down on the floor, her anger clearly visible.

"I hate that little Wiccan bitch." She said waving her hands in the air as she spoke.
"Yes dear Silvia, you've made it quite clear of your dislike for the young Miss Rhianlugh." Said Gavin, as he remained in the same thinking position, unresponsive to the rantings of his lovely minion.
"So why won't you just let me kill the little wench?"
"My dear Silvia, must I yet again remind you of how important she is to my plan?"
"No master, but how long must we hide our true intent?"
"Just until the night of the full moon when Miss Rhianlugh's powers are finally released."
"Please forgive my ignorance master but how will you manage to convince her to accept her powers? She's so far all but embraced them."

Gavin did not respond to the woman's question, his eyes now fixed on the moon which shown through the large window. The night sky played host with its clear darkness allowing the moon to shine like the brilliant beckon that it was. Silvia continued her pacing but was now silent, her wings now folded backward which meant she was a bit calmer than in previous moments. She dare not pursue her argument for fear of suffering her master's wrath, so she remained silent still pacing but carefully observing her master's facial expressions as he pondered his thoughts.

After several moments, Gavin arose from his chair, his shirt slightly wrinkled from sitting in one spot for such a lengthy amount of time. He fixed his gaze on Silvia who now was motionless in front of the large oak desk.

"Silvia darling, I need some suitable attire for tonight."
"You will be attending the social gathering as planned Master?"
"Yes, and after this night, all will begin to unfold."
"And once you've completed your plans, then I may kill that little bitch?"
"You may have your fill of the Celtic Knights, but I lay claim to the lovely Anora Rhianlugh is that understood Silvia?"

The slender faerie paused for several moments, realizing that her one waking thought, was just taken from her. Much as she wanted to personally drain the life out of her new adversary, she was honor-bound to obey her Master.

"Is that understood Silvia?" Gavin repeated once more, this time in a more commanding tone.
"Yes." She said trying hard to keep her anger at bay.
"Now pick out something pretty and change your glamor, you'll be accompanying me as my date darling."
"I will prepare for the evening's festivities Master and your attire will be ready when you are."
"Thank you Silvia, you are indeed a valued asset."

The slender faerie proceeded to exit the room, pausing only for a moment to turn and blow a warm kiss to her master. Gavin closed his eyes and allowed the faerie's magickal kiss to touch him. He could taste warm honeysuckles and sweet nectar upon his lips. A smile graced his face which gave the faerie confirmation that her kiss was welcomed. The wooden and brass door closed behind her, leaving the man alone with his thoughts. Gavin reached into his pocket and pulled out a small silk piece of neatly folded cloth. He laid the cloth on the arm of the recliner and began to unwrap it, revealing several strands of auburn hair.

Ever so gently, he picked up the silk cloth which cradled the strands of hair and placed it close to his nose, breathing in the sweet smell of the person for whom the hair once belonged to. He closed his eyes and began recalling the moments which led to the opportunity which allowed him to relieve the owner of their hair.

"She never suspected." He said to himself, still holding the cloth with the strands of hair close to his face.

"I will have you Anora, I will see my goal and my intimate fantasy realized. Once I have you." "I will have your powers and thus access to the Grand Grimoire, and once the Old Ones have been freed, I will be the God of the Witches."

Silvia opened the door and peered in, a smile draped on her face. She looked in Gavin's direction and licked her lips.

"Your bath is ready master." She said still smiling.

Gavin walked over to the door and opened it wider to reveal a naked Silvia on the other side. Her wings were folded inwards so that her hour-glass figure was in full view. He took her hand and brought a smile to his face. Picking up the slender woman, making sure to be careful not to harm her wings, he carried her off to the large bathtub, turning only to quickly glance at the still opened office door. He stared at the knob, willing it to come towards him. The knob turned slightly then proceeded to obey taking the rest of the door along until it was closed shut.

With the young lady fae in his arms, Gavin walked slowly down the small hallway towards a lacquer-finished door with a brass knob covered with fancy carvings. As they approached the door, the knob began to turn and the door opened wide revealing a large oval shaped tub filled to the brim with water and bubbles. The bathroom except for the large tub housed the usual items as most bathrooms, the smell of lavender and vanilla filled the air. Gavin stopped at the edge of the tub and gently lowered Silvia in, her wings immediately covered by the scented bubbles.

Gavin began to remove his clothing, his eyes fixed on the naked faerie in his tub but his thoughts were elsewhere. He visualized that the woman in his tub was that of the one whom he truly desired, naked and awaiting his company amidst the warm water and scented bubbles. What had started as just one man's attempt to gain power now had become one man's passionate obsession. He was down to his boxers now, still visually fixed on Silvia who was now display gestures of yearning and lust for her master. Gavin, still thinking of another, removed his boxers to reveal the already growing member underneath. The site of this widened Silvia's eyes as she licked her lips with satisfaction and hunger.

"I am ready master please take me." She said.

Gavin stepped into the mini pool-sized tub and faced Silvia who was now covered completely in bubbles, her skin glistening with the water upon it. Gavin had clearly heard the voice of his faerie assistant, but in his mind, he heard those words uttered on the lips the new object of his desires. The more he thought of him next to her, touching her, the more he wanted for his dream to materialize into reality. He grabbed Silvia with both hands and trusted her close to him. she could feel the full length of him against her abdomen which caused her to let out a breathy moan. The water was warm and the bubbles covered the upper layer of the large oval-shaped tub. Gavin looked down at Silvia, her eyes shown the colors of brown and gold autumn leaves. He placed his arms underneath hers and gently lifted her up, placing a soft moist kiss on her lips.

Silvia shivered, her body grew tense. She leaned into the kiss probing Gavin's mouth with her tongue. Gavin's hands found her buttocks, he gripped them tightly and with one fluid motion, he picked her up. Silvia's legs immediately wrapped around his waist as the kiss continued without interruption, she shivered once more as the tip of Gavin's manhood found its way inside her. She gripped him tighter with both arms and legs thus causing the rest of him to enter her. He had reached his fullness when he entered her completely and it did not take him long to find his rhythm. He gripped her harder, using her body as leverage as he thrusted repeatedly, making waves in the water all the while continuing his sexual onslaught on the young female fae.

Silvia's wings flung opened as waves of sexual sensations bombarded her body. She let out a series of pants and moans in acknowledgment of Gavin's actions upon her. Gavin paused and lowered Silvia down into the water, motioning her to turn her back towards him. The fae did as motioned, her wings still slightly opened and wet from being lowered into the water. He placed a hand on her back between her wings and pressed downward signaling for her to bend forwards. Again, she did as was instructed.

Silvia had only the edge of the tub in which to brace herself on, no sooner when she found her footing did she feel Gavin thrust into her from behind. Silvia's breath escaped her with ever thrust as the sensations began to build within her once more. She cried out Gavin's name but still his mind was more on his fantasy rather than who was bent in front of him. In his mind, he saw another bent over in front of him, her hair resting across her back. To him, Silvia's cries were her cries. This brought him to thrust even harder and faster the water in the tub becoming wavy once more. The tightness of Silvia and the warmth of the water brought Gavin to a thunderous climax. Silvia could feel the rush of warm fluid inside her, which brought a strong scream from her lips. Gavin bent forward resting his head upon her back leaving himself inside of her until he could regain his strength.

"Thank you, master, that was incredible." She said resting her head on her arms along the edge of the tub.
"The pleasure was indeed all mine dear Silvia."
"Forgive me for saying master." She continued. "You fuck like one of my kind."
"I'll take that as a compliment." He said as he backed away from her, releasing himself from within her body and started to make his way towards the edge of the tub.
"Yes it is the highest of compliments master for only those of my kind have proved satisfying until I met you that is." She said as she too rose from the water and onto the edge of the tub.

Silvia stepped out of the tub and walked over to where Gavin had stopped and was drying himself off with a large soft towel. Instinctually she reached out, grabbed the adjoining towel, and proceeded to dry herself off paying careful attention to her wings.

Gavin wrapped his towel around his waist and leaned over to kiss his faerie assistant on the cheek, his way of thanking her for yet another job well done.

"Now my dear shall we head over to the festival?" He said as he began to walk out of the bathroom.

Silvia wrapped her towel around her lower body and held part of it over her breasts as she followed Gavin out the bathroom. As they walked down the small hallway to the bedroom, he turned to her and smiled.

"Perhaps it would be best to change your appearance, after all, you and Anora didn't exactly get off to a good start." He stated, still wearing that grin.
"But what will you tell her?"
"Simple that Silvia has been relieved of her duties temporarily and you are her replacement."
"Then I will need a whole new identity master."
"Nothing we can't fashion up before we leave my dear."

Gavin grabbed her hand and led her into the bedroom where she had laid out tonight's evening attire for them prior to their bath. Silvia went in first and Gavin followed closing the door behind them.

Chapter Ten

It was a beautiful night, clear skies and plenty of stars both played host to a luminescent full moon. The air was cool and filled with the smell of fresh flowers and leaves, which hung from the surrounding trees. We were celebrating our annual Midsummer Night's festival and as always, everything was set up with the utmost attention to detail. The community square was ablaze with lights and decorated with bales of hay, wood-carved statues, white streamers, and baskets filled with fresh fruits and flowers.

The night air was cool and comforting against the skin. Everyone was full of anticipation for the upcoming festivities. There were tables with all sorts of foods, large barrels of red cider stacked by each table, and a large barbecue pit just adjacent to the community hall where the Midsummer's dance was to take place. Croix and I had returned from my interesting day at the office. By the time we had parked in front of the house, I was already removing my damp clothes. We had no sooner parked and turned off the engine when Aunt Ellice, Uncle Adler, and Gretchen Wilks came running out the front door. Uncle Adler had that stern look on his face which meant that he was worried. Aunt Ellice did not bother hiding her concern. Somehow, they already knew or had some idea that something had occurred. I remember Aunt Ellice's first words as she ran up to me and immediately hugged me.

"Anora are you alright you look a fright."
"I'm a bit shaken up but otherwise fine Aunt Ellice." I said smiling.
"I knew you shouldn't have left this morning." Exclaimed Uncle Adler who then walked over and hugged me as well.
"I still have to work Uncle, and I'm not going to put my life on hold like some frightened victim either."
"Well, the main thing is that you're home and alright." Said Aunt Ellice.

Yes, I was home and I was alright this time. At least one thing now makes sense, there is more to Mr. Gavin McLellan then just your average businessman. In addition, that assistant of his Silvia is defiantly more than she appears. I realized now that Gavin liked me more than I cared for him to and Silvia hated me just as much. Gretchen Wilks never spoke, she instead just looked at me from top to bottom with a stare that gave me the impression she knew what had happened, who or what did it, and how.

After telling my story and receiving those words of relief and support from my Aunt Ellice and Uncle Adler, I gave Croix a hug and went into the house to change clothes and take a well-deserved nap. I could not get my head onto the pillows fast enough before the sweet bliss of slumber overcame me. I was out like a boxer in a title fight. When I awoke, daylight had disappeared and the dark curtain of night had blanketed the sky. Three days have passed and I finally had an uninterrupted sleep.

It was warm outside, the cool breeze gently brushed across the land swaying trees and tall flowers in its path. I decided to give my legs some breathing room and adorned a nice off white sundress with a wide opened neckline and soft matching flat shoes. My hair was down and out so that it would flow when walk against the wind, a real turn on for most of the men in our community both young and old if I may add. Something told me that tonight was not going to be like the previous festivals but as for what exactly would make this one stand out from the rest was still unknown.

"Anora are you alright child?" Said Gretchen Wilks.

She had walked up beside me without my knowing, a clear sign that I was far away in thought, not something I should be doing given the circumstances. I looked over at the short elderly woman and smiled my usual "Everything's alright" smile but I knew she could see right through it.   The more I learned about Gretchen Wilks, the more I became convinced that there was just a bit more to her then she would lead us to believe. Music rang through the air as we approached the town square. People had gathered around smiling, laughing and conversing.

The local merchants had set up tables with all sorts of works from pottery to garments, it was truly a magickal night indeed and I felt safe and happy for the first time in days.

As we approached the center of the square, we were greeted by Croix and the rest of the Celtic Knights. They were in preparation for their ceremonial march through the square. They were dressed in their full ceremonial attire which consisted of black loose fitting pants, black boots and a semi-long robe which buttoned on the right side. The tops of the robes had hoods attached which they would drape over themselves during their march. You see we get a lot of tourists during this festive season and one of the main attractions is the march of the Celtic Knights. During the march, they summon their inner auric energy and focus it through their eyes causing them to glow. The crowd simply loves it.

Some communities frown upon such displays merely for the pleasing of visitors but we view it as a way for us to entertain while at the same time practicing on improving our psychic skills. Of course, we never show off our real magick like shape-shifting. Most of our community is made up of what people would refer to as your "average Wiccan" being that although they have the ability to tap into the magickal energies around them, they are not magickal beings like Kiedan and Tiegan thus some skills are forever out of their reach, at least in this lifetime.

"How are you feeling Anora?" Croix asked as he fastened his robe.
"Much better after having a nap." I replied.

Kiedan was walking over towards us. I could sense that he had something on his mind which he wanted to share with the rest of us. Tiegan and Kiedan were identical twins but you could tell them apart from the little differences about them. Kiedan was the more serious of the pair, I guess that's from his father's side whereas Tiegan was more down to earth and a lot more humorous then his brother. I remember growing up he'd call me Anora Borealis. He never teased me like regular kids did, but then again we weren't regular kids either.

I became comfortable talking with Tiegan over the years and could always count on him to make me smile. But it wasn't Tiegan who was approaching but his brother, Mr. Serious and I don't think that what he was going to say would make me smile.

"Merry meet Anora, Mr. and Mrs. Rhianlugh, and to you Elder Wilks." Greeted Kiedan as he stepped up to us.

We all smiled and gave a gratuitous nod acknowledging his formal greetings. Like I said, Kiedan was the most serious twin, big on formalities and short on humor. Gretchen Wilks simply stood looking at both Croix and myself with that "you're guilty" stare. I guess she wanted us to explain the story again so that Kiedan could be brought up to speed, but I didn't want to go backward, I needed to move ahead and find out some things especially his sudden interest in me.

The air had turned cooler as nightfall made its debut. There were the sounds of music and conversations from different groups of people in the town square. It was a beautiful night and I had almost lost myself to the moment when out of nowhere a voice called my name. I turned in the direction in which the voice had originated to find none other than Gavin and a young lady walking towards us. Gavin was dressed in a casual summer-like outfit of white with black shiny loafers and a black belt. The mysterious lady on his arm was wearing a low cut sundress of white. I guess she meant to compliment him by wearing it. Gavin's smile grew wide as he came closer to where we were standing, his eyes appeared fixed on me, lucky me. The two stopped mere inches from me. I could suddenly feel a tingling sensation touching my body, one of them was using magick.

My mouth started to feel dry and the sounds of the crowds seemed to become more distant almost to a whisper. I thought to myself that there was only one kind of magick which could do this to me so quickly and effectively, Faerie magick. I looked in the direction where Gavin was standing and I noticed that he was peering at me out of the corner of his eye. My body began to tingle and everything started to look hazy. I felt my mouth move but I didn't hear any words, I needed help and fast.

Croix looked right at me but appeared to not notice my condition which could only mean that whoever was using Faerie magick on me was hiding it underneath a very powerful glamour. Looks like I'm on my own at this point. I closed my eyes and whispered into the darkness "Goddess help me." I whispered to myself. My body started to shiver but not from cold, but rather from heat.

Somewhere amidst the blanket sea of darkness, there was an energy which had found my body and invaded it. The energy ascended from my feet upwards past my legs. When it found my most sensitive region, it poured itself inside me causing me to let out a throaty gasp. The energy continued its way upwards, past my stomach and chest until it reached the very top of my head. By this time, my entire body was tingling from this energy which had now taken up residence within me. My eyes were warm when I blinked but otherwise, I felt quite good.

I took in another deep breath and released it, time to open my eyes again. When I did I was greeted by a strong flash of light so bright that it was as if I were looking into the very depths of the sun. When the flash subsided and I was allowed to see once more, I noticed everyone within the general area standing like mannequins, all of them fixed on me. Even Gavin was looking, however, his gaze bore a cross between shock and satisfaction. Everyone else continued to stare, saying nothing until finally I had to just ask.

"Why are you all looking at me like that?"

No one tried to comment, their eyes still fixed on me. I could still feel the tingling of the mysterious energy throughout my body but now it started fading as if a violent storm was finally calming down. My vision cleared up as I surveyed my surroundings.

The music had stopped playing, no more chattering from amongst the crowds of people, only one sound could be clearly heard, the sound of a woman in pain. I followed the sound until it led me to look where Gavin McLellan stood. On the ground was a female faerie, her wings and clothes were tattered as if they were burned away, there were bruises all over her pale body.

From the looks of it, one would assume that she'd been attacked by some wild fiery beast but she wasn't. Again I looked at the group of people before me and asked another question as if I really got a decent response from the first one.

"What happened?"

"Anora my dear how do you feel?" Asked Gretchen Wilks who was the only one that didn't seem to have a shocked look on her face.

"I feel fine but what happened?"

"Don't you remember anything?" She continued.

"I was standing here when suddenly I felt strange and everything when black. The next thing I knew I asked the Lady and Lord for help, there was a tingling energy throughout my body, then this."

Gretchen Wilks stepped closer towards me and laid a hand on my shoulder. The first touch sent shivers throughout my body and caused her to quickly remove her hand. After a few seconds, she again laid a hand upon my shoulder. I looked down at the little woman, my facial expression was that of confusion. Our stare was interrupted by the once more shrieks coming from the injured faerie still lying on the ground. Croix stepped towards me and also laid a hand on my other shoulder. "Lady and Lord what did I do?"

"Anora you attacked Gavin's assistant." Croix said as he pointed to the downed woman with semi-scorched wings.

"Yes she did but in doing so she exposed the woman for what she truly is." Stated Gretchen Wilks.

"But I don't know how I did it."

"You said you felt something happening to you is that right?" Gretchen asked.

"Yes."

"Then it's simple, Gavin's assistant was attempting to harm you through Faerie magick and you somehow retaliated."

I looked over at the injured Faerie and noticed that she was staring up at me as well. Her face had shown a mixture of both pain and anger as she tried unsuccessfully to hold back her tears. I went over to where she lay and knelt down to her level to look her straight in the eye.

Hers were a swirl of purple and gray, which resembled storm clouds swimming in a night sky after a lightning strike. I had a few things to say to her.

"Why did you try to hurt me?" I asked.
"Fuck off Wiccan bitch." She replied with a hiss to her voice, looks like she also has a few choice words for me as well.
"What have I done for you to wish such karma upon me?"
"You were born and that's more than enough reason."

I took a second quickly run through my mind in the hopes of finding some past memory that would have given me a better understanding as to the resentment that this Faerie had towards me. "Just as I thought nothing." I was about to ask my attacker's name when Gretchen Wilks interjected. She was not at all happy with what had just transpired and she clearly wanted answers.

By this time, most of the people regained their composure and slowly but surely started to breathe life back into the festival. When you have lived in a world of magick and magickal beings for so long, you tend to grow accustomed to some of the "goings on" that may present themselves. Gretchen Wilks fixed her stare on Gavin who was now kneeling next to the injured faerie. He must have felt the energy within her stare because he suddenly turned in the direction to face the little woman who might I remind you wasn't very happy.

"Mr. McLellan, I trust you have an explanation for your assistant's behavior?"
"I assure you, madam that I had no knowledge of this and I will get to the bottom of it as soon as she is attended to." He replied.
"Why didn't you inform the council that you had magickal beings under your employment?" She asked harshly. She was beginning to probe for information now.
"Again madam Wilks I had no idea that my assistant was a magickal being."
"You do realize that this will have some significance on your initiation request?"

Two healers arrived escorted by two of the Celtic Knights. It was our community's law that none of our healers was to travel without escorts. Why do you wonder? Because over the years, even back in times of war, that the one you protected from harm the most was the medic.

The same holds true today especially because most demonic and magickal attackers usually target the healers first for without them, there would not be anyone to tend to the injured during battles. Many Wiccan communities have fallen as a result of losing their healers.

Gavin stood up and stepped away from the fallen Faerie to allow the healers to tend to her injuries. He took several steps thus ending up standing almost face to face with Gretchen Wilks and myself. I was so preoccupied with what was going on that I had completely forgotten that Gretchen Wilks' hand was still on my shoulder.

Was she attempting to keep me calm? I looked around at the people who were not enjoying themselves at the festival. Thank the Lady and Lord that this incident did not spoil such a wonderful event. However, something was still wrong as I glanced at the small group surrounding the fallen Faerie and myself. Croix, Aunt Ellice, Uncle Adler and the others were still soft of staring at me. No one was speaking again but still staring and still, I wanted to know why.

"Is anyone going to tell me why you're all still staring at me so intensely?"
"Your eyes Anora." Said Aunt Ellice.
"And what's wrong with them?"
"Well there glowing and we can't see your pupils."
"What are you all talking about?" I said with shock in my voice.

My eyes did hurt a little but other than that I could see just fine. Nothing appeared out of the ordinary to me but something was definitely wrong because they all saw it. Even Gavin McLellan was staring but again in his stare was that hint of satisfaction and a large helping of lust. Gretchen Wilks removed a compact mirror from her bag and handed it to me.

I opened it up and looked into the tiny mirror only to my shock to see that my eyes were white as if the whites completely engulfed my pupils and yet I could still see. I stared into the mirror searching for my pupils but with no success. Everything was bright white and shining which I guess would explain the warm sensation I felt.

"Anora dear." Said Gretchen Wilks who again laid a hand on my shoulder.

"Yes."

"Don't you think it's time that you composed yourself dear?"

"But I am composed." I said even though I wasn't completely.

"Be that as it may, in the words of your generation, you're freaking everyone out."

"But I am composed." I said once more, my eyes still warm from the glow.

"Anora just close your eyes and think of something or of someone that will calm you." Explained Croix who finally stopped being shocked and became the strong Celtic Knight again. He stood next to me tall and stiff like a soldier and bodyguard once more.

For as long as I can remember, Croix has always been around our family. He's never talked much about himself to me at least but I know there's more to him than what he displays. When I was a teenager I used to go to the movies and the malls with him. He made a good date because when I was with him, rarely did I receive any "comments" from other boys. You know the type, the "hey baby nice tits" kind of comments. I used to feel sorry for the few bold ones who did make such remarks because no sooner had they finish the "hey baby", Croix was already in their face. Croix has been my friend and myself- proclaimed protector since I can remember and now more than ever I needed both aspects from him.

I did as he suggested and closed my eyes, took a deep breath, and slowly released it. I imagined my mother and father back with me, the three of us enjoying a picnic in the meadow on a sunny afternoon. As I reminisced about times passed I could feel the warmth within my eyes dissipate and the coolness beginning to return. After several moments of thinking about the good times with my parents and silently telling my eyes to relax, I opened them.

Judging by the looks on the faces of those around I assumed that my efforts paid off and my eyes were back to normal. I smiled at the small band of people who had gathered even closer around me. For that moment, staring into the faces of the people who mattered in my life, I felt safe.

Even as Gavin stood next to his fallen assistant while the healers tended to her injuries, I felt untouchable by whatever negative force would dare come my way. I hugged Uncle Adler, Aunt Ellice, and Gretchen Wilks. As for Croix, he received the biggest hug of all. I was safe for now.

Chapter Eleven

If you were to combine Mr. Miyagi, your sweet grandmother, and Merlin, you'd have Gretchen Wilks. She has always had a way of communicating with anyone on any level and yet she still maintains her unique style. Gretchen Wilks is our town's oldest Wiccan High Priestess and from the stories, which were told to me by my Aunt and Uncle, she's seen her share of supernatural phenomenon. Gretchen Wilks has always been close to every family within our community, from assisting with the births of their children, performing the Wiccan weddings of couples, to presiding over the deceased on their journey to the Summerlands. I guess you can say that she's the heart of our community.

The night sky was its usual veil of darkness, laminated by the moon, and what few stars shown bright enough to make their presence known. Everyone within the community was one more enjoying the evening's festivities and the initiation of several new community members was on once more. Judging by the laughter and music, which filled the air around the town square, one would find it difficult to believe that just moments ago an attack on my life was made and worst yet, I don't know why.

I searched my brain and pieced together everything that I knew thus far in the hopes of making some sort of sense out of all this. After carefully re-thinking everything that has transpired so far, there was only one common denominator in all this, Gavin McLellan. However, if he's somehow responsible for all this, then the big question remains unanswered, why?

I first met Gavin McLellan or Gavin, as he prefers me to call him, about a week ago when he and his assistant visited the Graphics Design agency where I worked, requesting our services for one of his business ventures. From the moment I met him I felt a strange power touching me like hands made of air.

It wasn't until moments ago while piecing events together that I realized the same energy I felt when we first met, was the same as the sex magick that was being used to torment me when I attempted to sleep. Let's not forget to mention his assistant Silvia attacking me for no apparent reason in the ladies' room and now yet another attack by another of his assistants. I'm starting to feel as if I'm being targeted for assassination or something but again why?

I needed to sit down and unwind. I walked over to a nearby bench and sat down. As I looked around the town square, my eyes were greeted by people laughing and talking, music had filled the night air with an ensemble of string instruments and drums. The children were playing and dancing like little pixies at a party. The sight started to help me feel more festive and relaxed. There was a hand on my shoulder but unlike the small hand which belonged to Gretchen Wilks, this one was bigger and more firm. I turned to stare into Croix's warm and inviting eyes. Something about his facial expression just made me give a big lip-stretching smile.

"Hey, there pretty lady." He said still smiling as he spoke.
"Hey." I said still smiling.
"I'd give you a penny for your thoughts, but as it stands now I don't have a penny."
"It's alright Croix, I was just trying to salvage this evening."
"We're going to get to the bottom of this Anora."
"I have my suspicions."
"What are your suspicions?" He asked.

I took in a deep breath and looked around at all the now happy people populating the square. I wanted to forget all of this if only for a moment and simply take part in the festivities but I knew that I was now obligated to give him an answer otherwise, he'd never leave me alone about it. "I might as well get it over with." I thought to myself.

"Something is telling me that Gavin McLellan is mixed up in this somehow but I can't prove it."

Croix stood motionless for a moment, his eyes now fixed towards the main hall where Gavin and the others were now congregated, preparing for the evening's initiation ceremony once more. I could almost see the wheels inside Croix's head turning at the idea that the guilty party could be so close and yet so far at the same time, because without concrete proof, we couldn't confront him directly. There was only one thing wrong with our assumption.

The person who has been tormenting me at night has been using air magick. To use elemental magick requires a lot of energy and presently, no human can physically or mentally handle that much power without either their body shutting down or going completely mad. Gavin didn't look as though he was suffering from either. Croix turned surprised eyes towards me. He had questions as I knew that he would. I took several deep breaths and relaxed on the bench.

"I can see his connection with his faerie assistants but as for the magick being done on you." He stopped short of ending his sentence.
"I know it sounds far fetched being that no ordinary human could perform such magick without consequences but what if he was trained?"
"That's a frightening thought because human beings who are not of magickal decent cannot handle such powers." He said with what could have been fear in his voice.
"But the real question is why attack me?" I asked as if hopefully he would somehow have the answer.

We stared at one another for several moments trying to figure out the answer to that burning question. The bell in the town square sounded signaling that it was time for the initiation ceremony to commence. Gavin and a few others were given ceremonial robes to put on over their clothing just for the initiation and were standing in front of the town altar. The altar was comprised of three stone slabs giving it the appearance of a large table. Adorned around it were freshly picked flowers and vines, a black and silver tapestry which displayed a picture of the triquetra in bright bluish—white, covered the top of the altar.

Atop the altar were two large wooden statues, one of a male the other a female. Candles, a brass chalice, an incense burner made of ivory, and various nick-knacks were also present. Clearly the town elders went all out this time.

If there's one thing that I can say about the community in which I live is that they know how to throw a celebration. Everyone was gathered around the stone altar. The council which consisted of my Aunt Ellice, Uncle Adler, Gretchen Wilks and several other town elders were position in a straight horizontal line in front of the altar. Standing in front of them, draped in light gray hooded robes, were the three new initiates joining our community, Gavin being one of them.

No matter how much I wanted to just pull him aside and demand he reveal his motives to me, I had to hold my urges for the sake of those around me who's lives could be endangered if by some chance my hypothesis were right.

The music stopped playing as all attentions were focused at those standing in front of the large stone altar. The injured faerie, who was disguised as Gavin's assistant, was taken to the town clinic to rest and recover from her injuries that somehow I inflicted. They've placed two Celtic Knights in front of her room for her protection as well as to question her when she's recovered. Gavin still stated that he had no idea his assistant was, in fact, a dark faerie and does not know why she'd attacked me. The crowd hushed when Gretchen Wilks raised her hands, the initiation ceremony was about to commence and yet I still couldn't concentrate fully on one particular thing. My mind was bouncing from thought to thought and doing it so quickly that it gave me the sensation of dizziness.

As the ceremony progressed, the new initiates were anointed, and the dedication ritual commenced, we formed a huge circle so to add our energies to the ritual. We all stood and watched as Gretchen Wilks performed the ritual anointing each individual new member including Gavin. For the most part, it was a beautiful event as it usually is but something didn't feel right to me.

The air felt a little hard against my skin and not the usual soft supple whoosh that would play on the tiny hairs of my arms. The sound of bells started ringing in my ears and as I searched for their source, I noticed that no one else appeared to be looking for them, which could only have meant that I was the only one hearing them.

As the invisible bells chimed, their sound causing ripples to glide across my body igniting sensations as they touched those "special" areas. I started to give into the feelings that were coming over me until finally I could no longer control myself and I let out a soft yet sensual gasp. I guess I wasn't as soft as I had hoped because no sooner had I brought my sensations out, Croix turned and stared with a look that could only be described as the "What The Fuck" face.

"Anora what's wrong?"
"Don't you hear the bells?" I asked still feeling the waves of energy across my body.
"I'm sorry Anora but I don't hear them, but I believe that you do."
"Yes I do but I can't tell where they are coming from and the sound is making me." I gasped once more from the waves of sensations caused by the ringing of the bells.

I didn't want to attract any more attention but it was becoming difficult to keep my composure. My legs felt flimsy as if all the bones in them had suddenly disappeared. I thought to myself that if I don't gain control of myself or, at least find a place to sit down, I'll surely fall. Croix was still standing next to me. I stared and concentrated on him. I needed to convey what I was feeling but not aloud. You have to appreciate telepathy in situations like this. I closed my eyes and visualized Croix's face in my mind. Once the image became clear enough, I thought of what I wanted to say and without moving my lips, I started speaking. I opened my eyes and looked in his direction. It didn't take Croix long to sense that I was attempting to communicate with him for he quickly turned to face me.

"Croix I feel my legs are about to give out from underneath me."
"Are you feeling ill?"

"I can't feel my legs and I keep hearing bells." I grabbed his closest arm and held myself up at this point.

"I still don't hear them Anora but I believe that you do. What can I do?"

"I need for you to hear them." I said still wobbling.

"But I don't hear them so how can I?" He asked.

I closed my eyes trying hard to hold back both the frustration I was feeling and the increasingly annoying sound of the bells, which continued to chime in my head. I visualized Croix's face in my mind and focused on the bells, I wanted him to hear them as I did so that I could at least know that I'm not going insane. Croix closed his eyes and concentrated on me. Once he opened up his mind to me he immediately heard the ringing of the bells. The waves of energy, which swept through my body started to sweep through his as well causing him to temporarily lose his balance.

"Oh shit." He said as he fell to one knee but managed to recover himself.

"You hear them now?" I asked still struggling to keep my composure.

"Yes, but how the hell are you standing?"

"Just barely I assure you."

The waves of energy brought forth by the ringing of the bells continued to ravage our bodies as the initiation ceremony continued on. We used all of our available concentration to stable ourselves enough so not to bring about suspicion by the rest of the coven but we had to get help, me especially because the waves were beginning to take their toll on my body in parts most intimate. I looked at Croix who was standing although barely as the waves of energy were now affecting him as well.

"We need assistance and soon." He said.

"We can't call on anyone without causing a distraction." I replied, still fighting the urges which the waves of energy were bringing upon me.

Croix took a deep breath and began to look around hoping to spot the source or more likely the person responsible for the magick which was attacking us. We did our best to hide what was happening to us from the rest of the crowd that was still watching the initiation ceremony. However, it was becoming increasingly difficult as the magick was getting stronger and our restraint weaker.

The initiation ceremony had finally concluded and the celebration portion was about to begin, thank the God and Goddess because Croix and I couldn't maintain our composure for much longer and we needed to find a way to repel these magickal attacks.

"I don't know how much longer I can fight this." I said in-between breaths.
"We need to cast a protection spell on ourselves but we can't concentrate long enough to do so." Said Croix.
"I can't even telepathically call for help."
"We're on our own for the moment Anora."
"We need to leave but I'm afraid to move." I replied.
"Perhaps if we combined our psychic energies, maybe we can, at least have enough strength to telepathically call for help."

We tried composing ourselves enough so as not to cause a distraction from the evening's festivities but we really needed some assistance as the magickal attacks were increasing. I could feel my entire body vibrate, every internal organ shaking with sensation. I attempted to steady myself against Croix's body and looked in the direction of the altar where I noticed that Gavin had eyes fixed on me.

The mere thought of him staring at me with such intent and lust was enough to cause my legs to buckle underneath the weight of my body and I fell to the ground knees first. Croix knelt down and attempted to cradle me in his arms when we were again bombarded by the waves of magick and now he too found himself on the ground alongside me.

"Anora are you alright?' He asked as he attempted to shake off the effects of the spell.
"I think so but I can't move." I replied in a low breathless voice.

"It feels as though our bodies are anchors." He exclaimed.

"Ok it's official, we need help."

"Wait a minute Croix, do you notice something peculiar about all this?"

He paused for a moment and started to look around the square at all the people who have gathered for the ceremony. We both looked at the great stone altar and then at each other. At that moment, it was as if we caught the punch line of some invisible joke but we weren't laughing. He then turned to face me as we both were still pressed on the ground unable to break free of the magickal hold, which bound us.

"No one has noticed that we're on the ground." He said.

"Yes, whoever has cast this spell on us has also sought it fit to hide us from the masses."

"They must see us standing and unharmed."

"Then we're on our own Croix, Lady and Lord help us." I sighed.

We sat on the ground unable to move as the waves of magick continued to bombard our bodies. I tried to rise, only to end up back on my butt feeling the warmth of the spell which held us down as it entered our bodies. The sensation caused me to throw my head back, part my lips, and release a throaty gasp. Although he was concerned about my safety, Croix couldn't help but look with that horny male syndrome stare. I'm sure he's fantasized about the two of us being intimate but his duty came first and foremost.

At that moment, we were once more battered by yet another wave from the spell but this time, it was just me who bore the brunt of it. Croix started to pick me up from the dirt ground when he saw that someone had noticed our situation and was watching with intense eyes.

"Anora you won't believe who's watching us." He said as he sat me up.

Before asking him, I attempted to look in the general direction
that his head was now turned with the hopes of figuring it out for
myself. Once I gazed upon the crowd of people, I could tell that one
face had been turned towards us. The feeling that came over me next
could only have been described as complete and utter horror for none
other than the posh Mr. Gavin McLellan was staring, eyes fixed,
directly at us. His facial expression held a combination of the lustful
hunger that a man would have for an object of his affections and the
sheer anger of a jealous lover. This was anything but good.

"Shit, I can't believe this." I said with the horror in my voice
that matched the look on my face.
"I don't understand Anora, why is he doing this to us?"
"I don't know but I have reason to believe he's been responsible
for the recent attacks on me."
"But you've never met him until recently right?"
"Yes, but something inside me feels that he's responsible."
"Well, this isn't how I fantasized being on the ground whit you
and personally, I've had enough of this." He said, his eyes now ablaze
with yellowish light.

Croix is a powerful Wiccan but he was also not too eager to
display his abilities. Something told me that tonight at this very
moment, I would bear witness to a fraction of what he was capable of.
I fixed my stare at the large altar to where Gavin was still standing and
smiling. He could tell that we knew who was responsible for the
recent goings on and yet his smile told us that he was not worried. I
then turned my attention back to Croix who now had become filled
with energy, his body radiating a steady warmth that played upon the
tiny hairs on my arms.

As Croix stood, I could see the intensity on his face as he stared
back at Gavin who still sported that confident yet sinister smile. I
wasn't too quick to join him since I, receiving most of the force from
the waves of magick, didn't trust the stability of my legs but Croix was
already standing and poised to confront our attacker. There was a
feeling of hatred emanating between the two men, I knew that this
wasn't going to end smoothly.

I started to wonder if I should intervene somehow. Should I try and talk some sense into at least one of the men before this turned into a blood bath? I started to recall the incident in the ladies' room back at the office with Gavin's assistant Silvia, an incident to which I still have no clue how I managed such a feat.

Although I still had no understanding as to why all of this was occurring, one thing was certain, Gavin was behind it. One question answered, several more to go provided I survive the attacks which preceded them. For now, I needed to focus on the immediate problem as Croix had now made his presence known to Gavin and by the look on Gavin's face, he'd silently accepted the challenge.

"Croix don't! At least not here." I pleaded but it seemed to have fallen on deaf ears.
"No Anora, this ends now before it gets any worse."
"I agree but have you forgotten where we are?"

He paused for a brief second and panned around the town square looking at all the people who have gathered. To them, all seemed normal, but to us, they were suspended in time unaware of what was going on. Gavin was the only individual who seemed unaffected as we could see him shift moods from serious to joyful and back. He was existing between both planes at the same time. "What sorts of magicks were we up against?" I wondered. Something tells me that we were about to find out.

Chapter Twelve

If I was to be killed tonight, I at least, wanted to know why. For days, I've been the focus of magickal attacks and now this stranger, Gavin McLellan, comes into my life both professionally and personally and he seems to have his sights set on me. Well, at least I have an idea as to who's responsible for these attacks but I needed to be absolutely certain and I needed to find out quickly since both Croix and I were the subjects of this man's most recent magickal attack. We were standing in the town square as was everyone else from our community, all enjoying the festival of initiation when all of a sudden, I head bells ringing and waves of energies began lashing at my body causing me to topple over, eventually falling to the ground.

Thanks to the wonderful world of telepathy, Croix finally heard my cries and attempted to come to my aid. But coming to my rescue has also made him the focus of this most recent of magickal onslaughts. Soft white clouds covered the blue-black sky and the smell of cool spring water filled the air. Concentration is one of the most important aspects in magick and without it most spells will lose their potency so we silently agreed that we had to somehow get Gavin to lose his focus on the spell. However, what could we do, shy of me undressing before him, that would cause him to lose focus? We also had to consider that we were just about immobilized from the constant bombardment of magickal attacks. Croix turned towards me once more with eyes partially opened, the pain beginning to write its epitaph upon his face.

As strong as he is, Croix was starting to feel the strain from the magickal onslaught. We needed a way to stop this before it was too late. My body felt as if it were being put through a clothes ringer. All of my sensitive areas were inflamed and throbbing with pain. I was long past the pleasures that I initially felt when this had begun. I closed my eyes and with my inner voice I cried out for help.

"Lady and Lord your child of Wicca beseeches you for your assistance."

Croix must have heard me because the look on his face had changed. Even with all the pain he was experiencing, he still managed to show a hint of support as if somehow he knew that my prayers would be heard and answered. I hope he was right because my body wouldn't be able to withstand much more of this. The air around us grew warm and thick like a blanket forged by Mother Nature herself. It encompassed us. I began to feel the waves affect my body with less force each time they hit as if the invisible blanket of air was shielding our bodies from the attack. Croix and I exchanged looks, both noticing the strength returning to both our faces and bodies. We looked at Gavin who was now showing a look of sheer disgust and border-lined concern. The waves grew less in intensity until within a matter of moments, they had ceased altogether.

With all that was happening to us, we didn't realize that the first part of the imitation ritual had concluded and Gavin, along with the other new community members, were now the focus of a line of greeters and well-wishers who were shaking hands and giving hugs. No one noticed a thing as if Gavin, while attacking us, had also covered us in glamour. As we writhed in pain, those around us probably saw two healthy images of us, standing and smiling throughout the initiation ritual.

"If only they knew", I thought to myself but perhaps it's better that they didn't. When we were certain that Gavin had ceased his magickal attack on us, I once more closed my eyes and using my inner voice, thanked the Deities and asked if they would remove the protective covering. A rush of cool air ran past us, taking the invisible blanket of warm air with it. We could move freely once more and to our surprise, our bodies retained no visible remnants of what had happened. For the sake of those around us as well as having to explain the goings on which were unnoticed by the masses, we pretended that all was well and took two places in the greeting line. Croix was behind me but close enough to whisper words into my ear as we ventured closer towards the new initiates and to Gavin.

"It's going to take everything I have to not kick that bastard's ass for what he just did to us." He said in a low breathy tone.

"Normally I'd second that motion but we still have questions which need answering, and something tells me he's got them."

"The biggest one being why." He stated as we stood mere feet away from the new imitates including Gavin.

"He knows that we won't confront him in this crowd so for now we'll play along." I added as we were now standing in front of the new imitates.

We started down the line of initiates, shaking hands and giving hugs of welcome. I was first to approach Gavin and I stared into his face. His eyes held a hint of anticipation and glee. His smile looked genuine and sincere as he waited for my greeting. I proceeded to give him a smile back, holding in the anger and discuss as best as I could but my eyes must have betrayed me.

"We meet again dear Anora. You cannot imagine my delight." He said as he stretched his hand forward initiating a handshake.

"Indeed Mr. McLellan, and welcome to our coven." I said as I stretched my hand out to meet his for a quick handshake.

"I am truly looking forward to seeing more of you." He replied, his hand holding mine in our handshake which in my mind had ended moments earlier.

"I can't see why, I'm just your ordinary female Wiccan and there are more "unique" individuals in our community worthier of your communication."

"Indeed, however, I find you quite interesting none the less." He said with that same smile that he displayed when I was first introduced to him at the office.

I drew back from the handshake and gave my most convincing false smile. Croix was now in front of the man's face staring, his expression was genuine to say the least. He wanted to kill him. Gavin, feeling the strength of Croix's stare turned to face him. Neither man would risk a confrontation in front of everyone on this special occasion but they both made their feelings towards the other perfectly clear. It reminded me of my confrontation with Gavin's assistant in the woman's bathroom.

I watched the two men hoping that Croix's lust to destroy Gavin wasn't stronger than his resolve. I could feel the lump of air in my throat sitting as I waited for the outcome. Croix turned briefly to look at me; it must have shown on my face how worried I was. He gave me a quick smile and turned back to face Gavin.

"Welcome to our community." He said shaking the other man's hand firmly.
"Thank you, it's a pleasure to be here." Replied Gavin as it was clear he was matching the force of Croix's grip.

They released their hands and Croix began walking towards me while Gavin stood smiling and resumed shaking hands with the remaining townsfolk. Truly a close call if I do say so. Croix came to stand in front of me, his face radiating the emotional discuss that was once hidden when he shook Gavin's hand.

"I can't believe the nerve of that guy." He said holding the fist of his left hand into the palm of his right.
"I know but we can't get into it with him now.
"There's clearly more to him than he's showing and it's what he's not showing that's bothering me." He continued.
"We would do well to keep a close eye on him." I replied.
"Did you feel the energy when he shook your hand?"
"Yes I did, it felt a little dark as if he were masking dark energy with light but how?" I said.

Croix looked at his hand, "Yes he's clearly hiding something dark and sinister."
"We need to inform the Elders as soon as possible." I replied.
"Your Aunt and Uncle should be made aware Anora since they have firsthand knowledge as to your recent situations."
"Yes, I agree but after the festival." I said.

The night sky was a crisp black and bright stars danced across it creating a natural light show above us. The festival was now in full swing with food and entertainment. Croix and I watched as Gavin made his way through the crowds of people, shaking hands and engaging in idle conversation.

Gavin was a tall man about six feet five inches to be exact with one of those types of bodies that I refer to as sexy senior meaning he's well built for a man of his mature age which from the application he submitted at the Graphics Design Studio, was 56 years old. He was clean shaven and sported a well-groomed head of sandy blonde hair. He has the gift of gab judging by how he was working the crowds, engaging in all manner of conversational topics. I guess one would consider him the "ideal man" and yet, there was something about him, just below the surface that was dark and sinister in intent. Scary thing was that it had it sights set on me.

Although the thought of someone stalking me for whatever reason was disturbing in itself, I wasn't going to allow it to consume all of my time. I owed it to myself and to Croix to at least make an effort to enjoy the festivities tonight. It was clear that Gavin wouldn't do anything to me out right with so many eyewitnesses present so all I needed to do was to magickally protect myself as best as I could. Croix was still at my side determined not to let me out of his sight as we walked over to one of the nearby food tables. After all, a lady has to eat. If nothing more, I needed to keep my strength up. I reminisced back to my first encounter with Gavin and the incident in the women's bathroom with his assistant. If I am to fully combat any future attacks against me, then I had better keep my strength up.

I did my best to put a steady smile on my face so as not to attract any unwanted inquiries. Croix and I looked at one another and checked each other's smile for authenticity
which in doing so, brought on genuine ones from the humor of it.

"We must look so silly trying to falsify our smiles like this." He said quietly enough that only my mind's ear could hear.
"Yes, I bet we do." I replied telepathically.
"Do you want to speak with your Aunt and Uncle now?"
"No, let them all enjoy the festivities, in fact, we should take a lesson and enjoy ourselves." I said sporting a now genuine, semi-flirtatious smile.

By now the festival was in full swing, people singing Celtic songs and dancing the old dances of traditions past. There were elders demonstrating their various psychic abilities and giving lessons on rituals. Some were huddled in corners exchanging information on spells and invocations. Croix and I were finally beginning to enjoy the evening. I stood in front of the food table and took a bite of a piece of Witches bread. The sudden taste of cinnamon and wheat filled my mouth and brought on warm sensations of joy. It's only fitting that they named this bread Happy Wheat Bread. Croix and I stood munching on the warm bread and occasionally sipping on some Witches brew to wash it down.

I started to feel less nervous and much calmer as the time progressed, trying not to constantly focus on Gavin and the goings-on of the past few days. My body was finally catching up with my mind and became more relaxed. I noticed two tall dark figures approaching us from across the courtyard. Kiedan and his twin brother Tiegan were headed our way.

Kiedan was carrying a black hooded cloak with gold Celtic designs on it, whereas Tiegan held a shiny silver staff in his left hand, and his right was in the air waving at us. From the distance, I couldn't make out the details on the staff but something inside me knew that was the ceremonial staff of the Celtic Knights. It was in that moment that I realized they were coming for Croix.

"Croix we've been looking for you." Kiedan said as he stopped in front of us.
"Damn I forgot about the demonstration."
"Well we brought your cloak and the staff to save time but we need to get going, the others will be ready to parade through the square with the book shortly." Explained Tiegan.

Croix turned to look at me, his eyes clearly gave him away that he was worried about leaving me alone and unprotected. I took his left hand and held it tightly while displaying what I hoped was as convincing a smile that I could possibly place on my face.

I didn't what him to worry but to be honest, I was afraid, afraid of the possibility that Gavin would try again to magickally attack me and I being powerless to stop it. But again that one word traversed my mind, why?

The Elders began to gather in front of the large stone alter once more while the multitude of people started to take residency on either side leaving a clear pathway. Croix and the others quickly walked over to the far end of the town's square where they gathered and formed a flawless line in groups of two with Croix in front holding the staff in his right hand. Next to him was an older gentleman with snow white hair and eyebrows to match, his beard held a hint of darkened highlights but for the most part, it was as white as fresh fallen snow.

His hands cradled a large book which looked to be hundreds of years old. The outer covering was of raw leather which showed years of wear. I stared at the large book with the feeling that I was in some way connected to it but that's absurd since only the Elders, High Priest, and Priestess have frequent access to the book. The rest of us only get to see it during festivals and specific rituals. None the less, I still couldn't help but feel connected to it somehow. I've been feeling a lot of things lately, some of which I wish I hadn't.

I wanted to take my mind off of everything that's happened up to this point for at least the remainder of the night with the hopes of possibly enjoying the festival. "Good luck with that happening." I thought to myself. I tried to focus on the festivities while my eyes were fixed on one particular individual, Gavin McLellan. The small parade of Celtic Knights along with the Elder who was carrying the book had finally made their way to the large stone alter. The Elder stood in front of the altar and the Celtic Knights, formed a straight single line, behind it displaying their strength.

The Elder who held the book stood next to the High Priest and Priestess as the new initiates were lined up on the far end of the altar facing out towards the crowd.

The thought of that man, Gavin, becoming a member of our community after what he's done to me thus far stirred up a nauseating feeling inside my stomach but then again by having him in our community, I stand a better chance of finding out exactly what he's up to.

But the thought still sickened me none the less. The second half of the initiation ritual had begun as one by one the new community members stepped towards the High Priest and Priestess to become dedicated to The Craft.

Once they have pledged their dedication, they were to then place their dominant hand on the book and repeat the Wiccan Rede. Once the initiation ritual has concluded we dine, dance, and mingle. Personally, I know all that I care to know about Gavin McLellan but unfortunately, there's more to him than meets the eye and I'm afraid that weather I like it or not, I'm going to find out real soon.

Chapter Thirteen

The night sky played host to a gentle warm breeze which had just enough strength to cause my bangs to lift. I watched as each new initiate was dedicated and then given the Wiccan Rede to recite. Gavin was next and the more I thought of him being so close to my personal life the sicker it made me feel. Gavin walked up towards the High Priest and Priestess and lowered his head as have all the other initiates before him had done.

I had no idea that the sickened feeling I now had would soon be dwarfed by the feeling which was yet to follow. The High Priest and Priestess had completed the dedication ritual on Gavin and he was ready to recite the Wiccan Rede. The Elder stepped in front of Gavin and held out the large book which laid flat atop his hands. Gavin proceeded to place his right hand, which I guess in his case was his dominate one, on top of the book. I started to hear soft voices as if they were being carried on the wind, hundreds of whispers bombarding my ears. The whispers grew louder until suddenly as Gavin laid his hand atop the book, they turned into screams. My inner ear drum pulsed and vibrated from the multitude of screams and shrieks which seemed to be coming from every direction amidst the Waning moon above. As I looked around the crowd, no one else seemed to be affected by them which led me to one conclusion, like the bells before, only I could hear them.

The sound of the screams filled my ears and flooded my head until even the simplest thought became difficult to focus on. I closed my eyes tight and using my inner voice I screamed back "What are you saying?" As quickly as they began, the screams suddenly ceased. The sudden quiet disoriented me for a moment and as I regained my composure, I heard what sounded like many voices but in unison this time.

"Beware for he who seeks to possess you for his evil needs." Spoke the voices.

"I don't understand, who are you and who seeks to possess me?"
I replied still using my inner voice so as not to draw attention to
myself even though anyone who was tuned into the psychic realm
would have surely heard me. Distractions got to love them.

"You are of magicks which reside within the Grand Grimoire."
The voices continued.

"And who is trying to possess me without my consent?" I asked
but something told me that I already knew who.

"He who possesses the Grand Grimoire, he whose hand now
rests upon us, the one who is here under false intentions." They
replied still in unison.

It wasn't difficult after that response to determine who they were
referring to since it was Gavin's hand that was currently placed upon
the book when they spoke to me. The Grand Grimoire which was
stolen from our neighboring community, was packed with powerful
spells from centuries past, just about anything anyone could imagine
could be accomplished with a spell or ritual from that book. But the
book wasn't something that one could easily possess for only the
Elders of the communities knew the words to recite which would open
the book without causing harm to come to them. You see the book
could protect itself quite well. But why would he want me if he
already has the Grand Grimoire?

If someone who hasn't been anointed attempted to hold the
Grand Grimoire, its covers would horribly burn their hands and that's
the book's nice way of saying "Hands off." So I couldn't help but
wonder just how Gavin would have succeeded in acquiring it unless he
had help, so I decided to see if our coven's Book of Shadows knew.

"Please tell me if you know how he'll try to use the Grand
Grimoire?"

"By possessing the one who holds the Sun and Moon within
them."

"Who is the one?" I asked.

"You will soon know the one and your world shall forever
change."

As I started to ask another question when a loud screech rang in my head piercing my ears. The sound was so high in pitch that my eyes started to water. I tried focusing on one thought, silence, repeating in my mind over and over. The screeching suddenly stopped and I instinctively looked up towards the great altar where Gavin had raised his hand from the book and was now standing on the other side with the rest of the new initiates.

"What the hell was that?" I thought to myself as my eyes stopped watering. The ringing had ceased, and I was once again able to regain my composure. Now that my mind was free to contemplate, I thought of what the Book of Shadows had said to me and given the recent events in particular, it didn't take me long to figure out that the book was warning me. Gavin has somehow stolen the Grand Grimoire. Now only two questions remained, what did he want it for and more importantly who was this person who had the Sun and Moon within them? I needed to warn the Elders, I needed to talk to Croix. Hell, I needed to seriously brush up on my protection spells.

The initiation ritual had concluded and the Book of Shadows was being escorted back to its secure holding place within the walls of our temple. The crowd was busy dancing and enjoying the foods and drinks prepared by their neighbors. The sounds of flutes, guitars, and mini drums filled the night air as people sang and engaged in conversation. I wondered over to a nearby wooden bench and sat down overlooking the section of the square where most of the people were gathered. I panned the area searching for Gavin's whereabouts as well as for Croix and the others just in case things got heavy. I closed my eyes and took in a deep breath of the cool crisp air when I heard footsteps coming towards me. When I opened my eyes, who other than Gavin himself was fast approaching, his face held the smile of someone who just received the best news of their life. I tried not to look frightened but deep down I was.

I suddenly found myself fighting for air but it wasn't due to a spell being cast on me, just my own set of nerves getting the better of me. I blinked several times only to now have Gavin's tall figure standing in front of me.

I could feel a huge lump in my throat and although every fiber in my body was screaming for me to run, I did what I thought was best. I looked up at the figure of a man before me who was holding a cup in his left hand.

"Hello, Mr. McLellan." I said in the calmest voice I could muster.
"I thought we had dispensed with the formalities a while ago." He replied smiling.
"Yes, you are right, my apologies Gavin."
"Now that's more like it, after all, we're now of the same community my dear Anora." He said putting emphasis on the word dear as if he wanted to emotionally charge the word and then direct it towards me like some sort of Cupid's arrow.

I gave the area another quick pan to see if perhaps Croix and the other Celtic Knights were back from escorting the Book of Shadows to its resting place. I didn't want to be alone with this man and recalling what those screaming voices, which claimed to be from the book itself, had warned me of him. If there was one thing about Gavin that I've noticed, it was that he had no trouble picking up women and with all the potential surrounding us, why is he so fixed on just talking to me? I believe in love at first sight but our first encounter was strictly business. My thoughts stopped suddenly as I remembered the sensations that I felt when Gavin first approached me in the conference room. It was just like those waves of sexual sensations, which has recently haunted my night's sleep. Could Gavin be responsible for those as well and if so, I'm left with the same question, why?

"Anora are you alright?" Gavin asked as he took a sip from his cup.
"Oh yes I'm fine thank you for asking." I replied, not wanting to get too chummy with him given the potential circumstances.
"I must say the people here in your community are very hospitable."
"Yes, we like to make visitors feel welcome." I replied, perhaps I shouldn't have said it quite like that.

Gavin flashed one of those smiles that men give when you've said or done something which they found satisfying. I knew I shouldn't have said it quite like that but it was too late to retract it now. I took one last drink and discarded my cup in the wastebasket next to the bench. Gavin took a sip from his cup, his eyes fixed on my face as if waiting to see how my mouth would move next. He wasn't the only one, so was I.

I really wanted some sort of distraction to come forth and free me from this extremely awkward situation. Gavin never seemed to take his eyes off me as if he were studying every part of my body and taking mental notes. Men have stared at me before but there was something in the way Gavin did it which brought chills throughout my body. He had ideas on his mind and it involved me. Just as I silently uttered the words "Lady and Lord help me please", out of nowhere came Croix my proverbial knight in shining armor accompanied by the twins Kiedan and Tiegan.

Suddenly I felt as if someone had removed invisible bands from around my neck and wrists as I stood up from the bench to greet my saviors. I gave the three men a lengthy embrace, even allowing Tiegan to rest his right hand upon my buttocks. Out of the corner of my eye, I could see Gavin still standing there but his expression had taken on an entirely different demeanor. He appeared calm and casual on the outside but with every embrace between the men who unknowingly had come to my rescue and myself, I could tell that inside he was beyond pissed. I was hoping that at this point he'd simply excuse himself and leave but instead he smiled and took a short step closer towards the three men.

"It would seem that the lovely Miss Rhianlugh has many admirers among the men of this community." He said still smiling but you could just taste the hint of bitterness in his words as they traveled through the air.
"Oh we love ourselves some Anora." Blurted Kiedan as he gave me yet another hug this time from behind, his arms crossed just slightly below my breasts.
"That's right." Added Croix and Tiegan as they both kissed my cheek.

The men must have sensed that their actions were making Gavin somewhat jealous, to say the least therefore, they were going to play this little game of testosterone domination to its satisfying limits. I was just relieved that they arrived when they did, so I went along with their little game as long as no one got too carried away that is.

"Well I hope that I too will become good friends with Anora." Gavin said. He was still maintaining a sense of composure.
"Well." started Tiegan, "Anora is very particular about whom she befriends."

I looked at the men who now became a wall of muscle, flesh, and bone in front of me, shielding the view that Gavin had once enjoyed. Nevertheless, something kept eating at me. I could not help but ask myself "Why is he still seemingly so calm?" Clearly he was not a match for the men who were now literally in front of him, and yet he remained as calm as he was earlier. That did not sit well with me and I'm sure it didn't with Kiedan, Tiegan, and especially Croix.

"Well then until I am awarded the pleasure of your company dear Anora, I'll take my leave." Said Gavin still smiling gently and maintain that level of calmness.

Gavin turned around as if he had taken professional modeling classes and started walking towards where the other initiates were standing, having drinks, and chatting. Ever since that first day when he entered the conference room at work, I knew he was the sort of individual who had little to no difficulty mingling and, this time was no exception as he stopped in front of the group of people and began talking and soon laughing along with them.

He was excessively confident as if he knew that there was nothing, which could stop him from whatever he was planning. We all stood looking at one another with the same facial expression, curious and yet concerned. I now knew who was behind all the magickal attacks upon me but I still did not know why. Perhaps if the book could tell me who was doing me harm, then maybe it could tell me why and better still, how to stop him.

To think I'll have to deal with him for another couple of weeks at work until the project which he contracted our company to do for him is completed. Now that he's a member of our community, this is what I consider being one sick pre-birthday present. I would have preferred lingerie.

Chapter Fourteen

I awoke to the glare of the sun peeking through the large window in my bedroom. Its rays hurt my eyes for a moment but the warmth seemed to give me the boost I needed to get my butt out of bed and prepare to greet the Midsummer's day. I sat on the edge of the bed and rubbed the residue from the Sandman out of my eyes. I grabbed my pajama pants, which were dangling from the footboard of the bed and put them on. As I stood up, I could smell the aroma of Aunt Elise's homemade hazelnut and cinnamon muffins. It was Saturday and today was a very special day for me. Today I turned the tender age of ten. I was looking forward to a birthday celebration with my family, but more so, for my mother and father who were going to take me somewhere, which they simply described to me as "special."

Ever since I could walk and talk, my parents have been educating me in the ways of The Craft. Where other kids in for lack of a better word, "normal" neighborhoods were playing with toys, I was either in the kitchen mixing potions or in the study learning levitation, meditation, and a host of other psychic skills. You see, not only do I live in a community whose inhabitants are Wiccans, magickal beings, or individuals with supernatural abilities. I am also a descendant of a long lineage of Witches. My name is Anora Rhianlugh and right now, I am the happiest girl in the world. It is my day and I can/t wait to get it started. I put on my robe and slippers and ran downstairs to the kitchen where my Aunt, Uncle and parents all were sitting, sipping tea and talking.

I went around the table, giving hugs and kisses to those in attendance. Aunt Elise pulled out an empty chair while my mother slid the plate of muffins in front of me. They were all looking and smiling. I reached out, picked up a muffin, and started eating while the adults at the table continued their conversation. Although the majority of my attention was focused on the taste of the muffin, I couldn't help but hear what they were discussing.

I glanced around the oval shaped wooden table at the faces that were once more peering and smiling at me.

There sat my mother Diana, my father Kernu, my Aunt Elise, and Uncle Adler. Mom was in her favorite sun yellow sleeveless sundress that she would wear on special outdoor occasions during the warm seasons. Dad liked that dress because of the amount of skin and cleavage it showed. Mom and Dad loved each other very much. It seems that everyone in the community knew it too. They were always seen together, either holding hands or engaging in a quick kiss. Dad had a job that only took him away from us for a few months and during that time, Mom would miss him but her wait never seemed to last too long and before we knew it Dad was suddenly back among us. It was happiness as usual until the next time he had to go away.

Mom never really elaborated on exactly what sort of job Dad did, just that it dealt with the preservation of the environment and the creatures who called it home. Besides taking care of me, which I for one think they did a damn good job. Mom, as far as I know, was a counselor of sorts. she'd receive calls from people all over who were followers of The Craft and she'd assist them in either their magickal works, personal problems, or various other needs that they may have. It was said that she was able to escort the dead to the Summerland's. All I knew was that I had the best set of parents that any child could ever dream have. They loved me with all their heart and I loved them.

Today was my birthday. I was finally in the double digits and that made it even more special. I sat at the table filling my face with Aunt Elise's muffins, listening to the sounds of my parents, Aunt, and Uncle chatting and laughing away. Life was good. It was about noon when we had realized that we'd been sitting around the table chatting, laughing and steadily consuming muffins. Mom looked at me and smiled that bright smile of hers. She could light up the darkest of places with that smile.

"Happy birthday Anora." She said as she stood.
"HAPPY BIRTHDAY ANORA." echoed the others from around the table.

I smiled so hard that my face hurt but I was happy. I couldn't wait to see what other wonderful things were still to come. My mother walked over and kissed me on the head as the others rose from their seats and Aunt Elise began clearing the table. Dad walked over and stood in from of me. He looked like a pillar of all things beautiful and earthly. He too bent down and kissed me on the top of my head.

"Well birthday girl are you ready to celebrate?" He said smiling.

"Oh yes I am father." I replied wrapping my tiny arms around his waist, pressing my head against the solidness of his abdomen.

Dad was tall and quite the husky type. His hair was deep black with perfectly precision streaks of gray. His face was sculpted perfectly with firm cheekbones, manly yet soft lips and a strong chin. Mom, on the other hand, was the epitome of beauty.

Her hair was near ankle length and a dark brown almost black but more so like Dark chocolate. Her face was soft with a small nose and moist pink lips. Both Mom and Dad had bodies that any adult would have killed for and yet they never really did anything close to normal exercise. I used to hear my Aunt Elise say to them that they were the physical representations of the Mother Goddess and Father God in that they were opposite but yet similar. They perfectly complemented each other. Really such high praise indeed but it wasn't just my Aunt and Uncle who viewed them in that manner, the whole community did as well.

Mom and Dad were the High Priest and Priestess of our community and on many occasions, others from the surrounding communities would come to participate in our seasonal rituals because of my Mom and Dad. I felt as if I had celebrity parents. Nevertheless, they always had time for me. Mom used to take me out to the meadow. There she taught me how to listen and speak to the trees and plants. She showed me how to feel when the seasons changed and how to harness the energies from them for use with my psychic and magickal workings.

Dad would take me to a large redwood tree that sat in a meadow down from our home, there he would sit on a stone slab beside the Great Tree and tell me stories of magickal beings and even a fairy tale or two. Sometimes, he'd give me lessons on how to defend myself both physically and magickally. I had all the love that a child could ever imagine and today, on this my tenth birthday, I was yet again thankful for the gift of my parents.

"Run upstairs and get ready sweetie." Mom said with a smile.
"Ok Mom I'll be right back." I replied as I darted up the stairs and into my room.

The sun was out in all its shining glory, lighting up a cloudless blue sky. It didn't take me much time before I had showered, dressed put on my white sundress with matching white flats, and descended back down the stairs to my awaiting family members. Mom and Dad were now standing at the door. Dad was holding a basket and Mom a large wooden box with a pentagram carved on the front. Aunt Elise and Uncle Adler were standing in the living room entrance.

"Someone looks eager to go." Said Uncle Adler as both he and Aunt Elise kissed me on my cheeks.
"Have a good time sweetie and we'll see you later for the festivities." Remarked Aunt Elise after pulling away from the kiss.
"Thank you Auntie and Uncle, I know I'll have fun with Mom and Dad and I can't wait to see you later for cake."

With that, the three of us walked out the front door. We took each other's hand with me in the middle and started our walk down the path towards the meadow. We took our time walking, holding hands and smiling. I was a kid high on life. "Nothing was going to ruin this day." I thought to myself as I looked up at my parents. In the distance, I could see the tall white lilies and sunflowers that were swaying in the summertime breeze. The large redwood tree towered over the meadow, standing firm and defiant. I wanted to reach the tree, yearning to sit beneath its mighty trunk. I let go of my parent's hands and started running. When I reached the base of the tree I stared upwards as high as my neck would allow, then with a smile, I greeted the giant redwood.

I wrapped my arms around the large tree as best as I could and pressed my body against it with one ear against the trunk trying to listen to the sounds of life from within. By now, my parents had reached me and were standing in front of the Great Tree, staring up at its high branches and smiling. The soft breeze ran through the limbs of the tree, causing its leaves to whistle. Dad laid out the large handmade picnic blanket and both he and mom sat down to unpack the basket. I held onto the tree for a little longer, closing my eyes and taking in its positive energies.

The wind seemed to transform into a much stronger, commanding howl, blowing my hair in front of my face. I couldn't see anything but when I tried to let go of the Great Tree, it seem to hold me fast against it as if it were in some way protecting me from whatever was happening. Amidst the rustling of the tree's limbs and the howling of the now seemingly gale force wind, I could hear my parents chanting. Whatever was going on, they were trying to thwart off. I wanted to look and see but the tree held me tightly against its wide trunk. The sound of thunder filled the skies and the once bright sunny afternoon was now dark and stormy. I was frightened but I didn't call out for my parents, something inside me told me not to. Deep down, I guess I knew that they were trying to stop what was happening and if I called out for them, it would distract them.

I heard another voice, deep and steady in its wording but I couldn't tell where it was coming from. "Come forth Old Ones and claim her." It said and with that the wind blew even harder as if there were a tornado touching down right where we stood. The smell of dead things invaded my nostrils causing me to gag but still the Great Tree wouldn't let me loose from its grip.

I heard my mother cry out "No you can't have her." I started to cry inside for my parents, I wanted to join them to help thwart off whatever evil was attacking. I heard my parents chant another protection spell or at least, that's what I thought it was since I had no knowledge of the dialect in which they were using. I felt heat on my back as they continued to cast.

The other voice was also chanting as well, and then in one split moment, there was a flash of light and continued heat then a loud horrific screech. The other voice screamed, "Damn you." And with that, silence filled the meadow.

The sound of birds suddenly filled the air, and through my eyelids, I could see that the sun had reemerged from the darkness. However, the tree still kept hold of me as if it knew that I was still in some sort of danger. I closed my eyes, took a deep breath and decided to do what I've done for years when visiting the Great Tree. I began to talk to it.

"My friend, why won't you release your hold on me?"

There was silence for the first few seconds then like a rumble of thunder the tree spoke in a voice deep with age and strength.

"The one who wishes you harm is still here."

Before I could even inquire, a hand grabbed my left shoulder gripping it on contact. I knew that it was man's hand by the size and strength but I didn't know if it was someone with good intentions or not. But the Great Tree knew, it held fast to its hold on me. "Release her, she is to be mine." Said the voice in a commanding tone. When he spoke I realized that it was the same person who was casting the spell to which my parents were trying to thwart and that pretty much told me all I needed to know with the exception of one thing. Where were my parents?

The man continued to tug at my shoulder, trying to pry me from the tree's grip. I heard rustling above me and looked up to see that the lowest branches of the Great Tree were moving downward towards me. The branches wrapped themselves around the man's wrist and began to wind themselves up his arm. The man cursed the tree and started to pull his arm away but the tree held fast ever increasingly tightening its grip on the man's arm thus causing him to let out a loud yell followed by several more curses. By now I just wanted everything to end and for my parents to scoop me up and take me home for cake.

"Lady and Lord help me" I thought to myself, then the sound of fabric tearing filled my ears as the man finally released his hold on me but at the cost of losing one of the sleeves to his hooded cloak.

The Great Tree pulled the man's arm one more time before releasing it, at which I could see out of the corner of my eye, a symbol tattooed on his forearm. Three swirling circles formed together to resemble a triquetra the eye of Horus above them. I blinked once and the image burned itself into my mind for all time. When I blinked again the man was gone, all that remained of him was the torn sleeve from his hooded cloak which was still in the possession of the Great Tree's branches. All must have been safe as the Great Tree finally relinquished its hold on me. I stood looking around for signs of my parents but to no success, they were gone literally vanished into thin air much like the mysterious man. There was only one thing for me to do, run as fast as my legs could carry me back home.

Once I started running, I didn't stop until I reached the front door of my home. Just before I could knock on the wooden door, it flung open and out, with arms outward, came my Aunt Elise. She held me close, spun us both around towards the opening, and hurried us both back inside to where my Uncle was waiting to close the door behind us.

When we were safely inside, Aunt Elise let me go just enough to stare at me. I took this opportunity to examine the faces of my Aunt and Uncle. Judging by the expression of both fear and surprise, I would suspect that they either already knew or, at least, had some idea as to what happened.

"Mom and Dad are they here?" I inquired.

Silence, as they continued to stare at me. It's as if they were surprised to see me in the first place but are they aware of what happened and if so, why won't they tell me about the whereabouts of my parents? Both Aunt Elise and Uncle Adler stared at one another but were careful not to use telepathy to converse amongst themselves as they knew I could hear them thanks to the psychic spells taught to me by my parents. They gave me another round of tight hugs and sat me down on the sofa.

"Dear child are you alright?" Said Aunt Elise as she stroked my hair.

"Yes but I don't know what happened to my parents. There was some sort of a magickal battle between them and a strange hooded man but I couldn't see anything."

"Ah your mother and father are stronger then you know, they'll be alright and I'm sure we'll see them real soon." Bellowed Uncle Adler who was standing behind me.

I told them everything that I could recall including how the Great Tree protected me but in doing so, kept me from seeing what happened to my parents. After I finished my recant, I paused to hear something from the two hoping they would shed some light on things. Again silence. They had no idea or did they? I took a moment to study their faces. Uncle Adler's expression took on that "fatherly" strong and protective look but in his eyes, I could see that he was worried about something. Then I turned my observant gaze towards Aunt Elise. "Bingo", I said to myself.

Her expression was that of one who was trying to hide one's true self behind that of a blank stare. She wanted to just tear up and cry. I didn't let on that I could tell. Aunt Elise was the first to speak after our brief moment of silence. I could tell that the next words from her lips would be difficult for her to voice.

"Sweetie, I'm sure your parents will be back soon",
"Yes you just have to be patient." Uncle Adler chimed in. Guess he didn't want her to have to go through comforting me all by herself, or perhaps he was just telling her in code that if need be she had his support.

We left the conversation at that as I was then told to go and wash for dinner. Later, I recall coming down to a hot meal and a cold glass of pineapple juice. Then suddenly feeling exhausted and being carried off to bed by Uncle Adler. All I remember to this very day was that my parents had mysteriously vanished after battling that strange hooded man. I've always pondered whether or not Uncle Adler and Aunt Elise knew what had truly happened to them and perhaps who that strange man was and what was he trying to do? Dreams can really help bring out memories which were conveniently tucked away by those who love you and claim to have your best interests at heart.

I guess that's the reason why they took such a parental stance since that day and practically raised me as their own daughter. After that day, I'd have fragments of dreams which until recently I realized were more than mere images from my subconscious, but in actually, were an account of the incident which took place that faithful sunny day. Now decades later, here I am, all grown up and about to celebrate another birthday. Yet once again I find myself wanting the same birthday gift, to have my parents back in my life.

It's late and everyone in the community appears to be fast asleep, all except of course the Celtic Knights who are on patrol. I'm still tired from all that took place and regardless of whether I remember what happened or not, I do know that I need to get some sleep. Pulling the covers over my head and closing my eyes, I bid good night to the Goddess and the God and said I love you to my Mother and Father.

Chapter Fifteen

The morning seemed to arrive more quickly than usual. Perhaps it was due to the quantities of drink which I had consumed after my encounter with Gavin McLellan. In any event, a new day was here and I needed to get ready for work. I got out of bed and did my one-two step into the shower, the one being I pulled off my night shirt and the two being me standing in front of the shower. I could always get dressed, and on some occasions undressed, at a moment's notice when the mood hit me that is. Today the mood hit me hard so I showered, brushed my teeth, and put on a pair of light gray pants along with a light pink blouse. I didn't bother to put on socks as the black casual flats I slipped on didn't require them. Before leaving my room, I walked over to my alter, and bid good morning to the Goddess and God, thanking them for letting me see another day.

As soon as I opened my bedroom door, I smelled it, Aunt Elise's hazelnut and cinnamon muffins. I descended down the stairs and into the kitchen where I was immediately greeted by Aunt Elise and Uncle Adler who was already partaking in one of Aunt Elise's muffins. As I sat down, Uncle Adler raised his head from his plate and looked at me. "Here comes the morning conversation." I thought to myself.

"Well my dear you seemed well rested given the aftermath of last night's celebrations." Said Uncle Adler.

Translation: "You don't look a bit hung over given the amount of drink you consumed last night at the festival."

"I feel good today, a new day and I'm fortunate to bear witness to it." I replied.

Uncle Adler won't admit it but he likes it when I get all "old school" Wiccan like that. It's kind of like those people who prefer to speak and be spoken to in Shakespearian.

"Anora dear." Interjected Aunt Elise. "Will you be home in time for today's practice's?"

At least three times a week, a few of us get together and practice our magicks together. We'll work on our spells, make sure we're reciting certain magickal chants correctly, and do a little psychic play. Aunt Elise and I usually partake in the chants and light spell casting, but things get much more fun when I get to practice with Croix, Tiegan, Kiedan, and a few others. We'll have magickal duels, at least until something accidently blows up that is. It's never intentional mind you, but after all Croix and the others are Celtic Knights and they have to be prepared for just about any and all sorts of magickal and non-magickal situations so there's very little room for "pussy-footing" around when it comes to magickal training.

"Yes Auntie, I'm only working a half day today as the company will be closing for the next couple of weeks while renovations are made." I replied, smiling with half a muffin occupying one side of my mouth.

Since the office was closing for the next two weeks for renovation, I wanted to get in there and finish up my projects so as not to have any "homework" as it were. I gulped down my orange juice, rose from my chair and gave both Aunt Elise and Uncle Adler a big hug and kiss on the cheek. Then in my one-two step fashion, I grabbed my bag and was out the door. I got in the car and started it up, immediately turning on the radio. There was the sound of my buddy Richard from WIC Radio. Traffic was surprisingly light but then again, it was the end of the week and most likely a lot of people choose to start their weekend early. "Wish traffic was like this all the time." I thought to myself. Shortly thereafter I pulled into the company parking lot. I parked, shut off the engine, set the car alarm and walked over to the large glass doors. It was quiet in the lobby, hardly anyone was around.

A security guard and a desk clerk were chatting it up at the front desk only to stop at my passing. I wasn't trying to read their thoughts but honestly, the look on their faces was enough to confirm what they were thinking as I strolled by.
"Damn the things I would like to do to her." Thought the guard who simply smiled as I passed by.

At least, the front desk clerk was a bit more generic. His mind only held one word, "Yummy." I got up to the elevator door when it suddenly opened.

Murray placed his hand on the door to keep it from closing as I walked in. He smiled showing all of those pearly whites which immediately told me that he was more than pleased to see me.

"Hey, lady how are you?" "You know you just gotta fill me in on all that went on at the festival?"

Murray is probably one of the most sophisticated and yet funny as hell gay men that I've ever meant. I could always count on him for fashion tips and the latest in company gossip. He gave me a big hug and pressed the 4th-floor button, then the chattering commenced.

"So tell me all the details." He said happily.
"Well the festival as a whole was very nice but you won't believe who joined our community." I replied as the elevator stopped.
"Who?"
"Gavin McLellan." I replied just as the elevator doors opened.

Murray's facial expression changed to a more frightening look as if I had just told him that something evil were after him. He clenched his fists and stared at me for a
moment, possibly searching for the right words to match his current state.

"That bastard was here earlier." He started.
"He said that our services would no longer be required as he and I quote "Got what he needed out of the deal." He took a quick breath and went on. "Then he handed Bruce a check and left."
"I wonder what he could have meant by that?"

Then like a sudden flash of lightning it hit me. Last night at the festival, the Book of Shadows had warned me that he possessed the Grand Grimoire which was stolen recently from a neighboring community and now this sudden dismissal of our services. He's covering his "loose ends" which could only mean he's either about to make his move or worse, he already has. I must have had an unusual expression on my face because Murray suddenly grabbed my hand, yanking me from the elevator just as the doors were closing, and held me close to him looking down at my still strange expression. I realized that I was lost in thought and quickly came back to reality which began by staring back up at Murray's face.

"Anora are you alright? You zoned out for a moment."

"Yes I'm ok, but I suddenly have a feeling that something terrible is about to happen and Gavin McLellan is involved." I said shaking with chills at the mere mentioning of his name.

We walked down the carpeted hall, past the women's bathroom where my encounter with Gavin's personal assistant Silvia Blakely took place. It had been repaired since then but I hear that the authorities are still questioning how it got that way. We arrived at the office door where the receptionist area was when we were met by Bruce. He had a blank look on his face but tried his best to smile as he approached.

"Ah Anora, I never get tired of seeing you." He said as he gave me a big hug.

"It's always nice to see you to Bruce." I replied.

"We're going to have a brief conference and then close up shop for the two-week renovation."

Craig and Delia were already sitting at the large conference table when we walked in. Bruce, as usual, took the seat at the head of the table while Murray and I took up the adjoining two seats. Only one vacant seat remained. Croix was not in attendance.

"Well as I'm sure you all know Gavin McLellan has terminated our contract, but not before leaving us with a nice compensation." Said Bruce.

"What did he mean that he got what he needed out of the deal?" I inquired.

"Beats the hell out of me, but one things for certain, he took all of the samples and documentation with him as part of the initial contract."

"So what does this mean? Are we done with the project at this point?" Asked Craig.

"Looks that way, but since he was the last opened project, at least we won't have anything waiting for us when we return in two weeks." Replied Bruce who closed his notepad at that point.

"Well off the record, I'm glad that we're finished with him, he gave me the creeps." Stated Delia.

"I second that." Retorted Murray.

"Well ladies and gentleman, unless there's anything else which needs mentioning at this time, I'd like to thank you for your hard work and enjoy your two weeks off."

We stood from the table and bid one another a fond goodbye. Delia and I went out of the conference room first, since we were the only ladies. I stood at the receptionist desk for a moment when Bruce suddenly approached me. He had that worried look on his face that I've come to know from our years of working with one another.

"Bruce what's wrong?"
"Anora I didn't want to discuss this in mixed company but there's something I wanted to tell you." He began. The tone of his voice was starting to worry me as it had a hint of fear in it.
"What is it?
"It's about Gavin. We had a brief discussion at his request in which he asked quite a few questions."
"About the project?"
"No Anora, about you."
"Me?" I shrieked. "What kind of questions did he ask you?"
"Believe it or not, he asked me if I knew your magickal abilities and if I've seen you in action, so to speak."

There goes that sudden flash of lightning again as I recalled something else that the Book of Shadows had said to me the night of the festival. Something about needing the one who holds both the sun and the moon within them. "That does it, I need some answers." I gave Bruce a comforting hug and drew back to look into his face.

"Hey don't worry, I'll be alright." I said in my most reassuring voice.
"I know you will Anora, but you can't blame a person for worrying anyway."
"No I can't."

He smiled that "I'm concerned but I don't want her to notice it" smile. Bruce has been my employer for close to ten years, and during that time, we've grown to have a close friendship with each other. He's been to my home for dinners with my family and I've been to his home for parties and get-togethers. We've never crossed the line between employee and employer by sleeping with each other, but I did let him kiss me on several New Year's Eve celebrations. For a stern and professional man, his kisses tell the story of a soft-hearted and sensitive soul. There were many times when he and I would sit and share the most emotional of stories with each other as we found comfort in one another's presence.

"Promise me one thing Anora." He finally spoke.

"Sure."

"Promise me that you'll try your best to be safe."

"I promise." I said and I laid a gentle kiss on his lips, not pressing as to invite intimacy, but enough to reassure him that I appreciated how much he cared.

I started down the hall towards the elevators, leaving Bruce where he stood. I think he was savoring that kiss. As I pressed the button and the doors opened, I heard Bruce call out to me one last time.

"I'll be seeing you bright and early in two weeks Miss Rhianlugh."

"Yes, sir Mr. Kirkpatrick." I said with a smile as I stepped into the elevator and the doors closed behind me.

It was just past noon when I got out of the elevator and walked through the underground parking lot to my car. I took out my handy keyless remote and pressed twice to unlock the doors. I sat in the driver's seat, closed, locked the doors, and there I sat for several minutes thinking of past events and the warning that the Book of Shadows had told me. I thought about the day when my parents disappeared and the events which took place, the hooded man who had summoned the terrible storm, and the Great Tree whose branches held me close protecting me. I thought about Aunt Elise, Uncle Adler, Croix, Tiegan and Kiedan, and for a brief instant, I thought about Gavin McLellan and all that has occurred as a result of his appearance. But what I didn't want to think about as I started the car and began to drive off was what awaits me from this moment on. "Lady and Lord help me."

Surprisingly traffic on the expressway was light. Probably because it was still early and if anyone was out, it was to grab lunch at a nearby eatery. All I could think about, and it sickened me to think it, was what Gavin might be up to. Why did he end the contract with the company before we could even complete the project? Why in the hell did he become a member of our community? But most of all, is he the one that the Grand Grimoire predicted would take it? More importantly, what does he plan on using it for? Damn, too many questions and not enough answers.

Ah, home, there's no place like it in the world to me. I always get a nice warm satisfying feeling when I drive up that dirt road towards our community. I didn't get half way down the road when I was stopped short by the appearance of a huge black wolf. The wolf stopped in from of my car and stared at me, its eye blazing with a yellow glow. I put the parking brake on and eyed the large animal waiting to view its next move. The black wolf launched itself upward to stand on its hind legs and within mere moments, there stood Tiegan.

"Anora I sensed you were coming." He bellowed standing in all his glory.

"It's always good to see you to Tiegan, but right now I'm kind of seeing more than perhaps I should don't you think?" I replied trying hard not to look at his lower extremities.

He looked down then back up at me and flashed what more humans would refer to as a million-dollar smile. I stepped out of the car and slowly walked over to where he now stood, slowly shaking my head no and smiling as if to say "You are just too much."
Once face to face I placed my left palm upon his bare chest and concentrated on him wearing clothes, and with one deep breath, I used the spell to clothed the naked.

"Adficient eum uestimentis." I recited and in an instant, he was adorned with blue jeans, a crisp black short sleeved shirt, black socks and black shoes. And of course, I did add boxer briefs just to keep the jewels in check.

"Oh, baby you sure know how to dress a guy up." He said with a chuckle.

"So what's the meaning for the greeting?" I inquired.

"Oh I get to help with your magickal training today and I got impatient, so when I smelled you approaching and I just had to come and meet you."
"I see." I replied.

"We need to get to your place, the others are waiting for you there."

"Others?" I said, my voice raising a couple of notches from its normal tone.

"Yes, apparently Elder Gretchen believes that something or someone of pure evil is coming and she wants all of us ready, especially you for some reason."

"What?" I replied, the look of surprise clearly showing on my face.

"Yeah, that's kind of what we all said when she announced it." He said.

He paused for a moment then looked down, his eyes partially opened as if he were ashamed of something. I reached over and placed my hand underneath his chin lifting his face up to meet mine once more.

"What's the matter?"

"Someone has somehow managed to steal our Book of Shadows." He finally uttered.

"WHAT!" I shouted in disbelief. The Celtic Knights are better at security than any human security force or agency. With their combined fighting and magickal skills, they have proven to be quite the formidable force. How could anyone even get close to let alone manage to steal the Book of Shadows? Up until now, it has been considered virtually impossible. I could tell that he was hurt by this so instead of bombarding him with fifty million questions, I did the next logical thing. I pulled him close to me and held him. We stood there for some time in silence as he tightened his hold on me, burying his face into my hair.

"Tiegan we should be getting back now." I said softly.

He slowly withdrew from our embrace to once again stand in front of me. I could tell by his eyes that he tried desperately to hold back tears but a couple managed to trickle down.

"I know that no one can get past you and the other Celtic Knights, so whoever took the book had to of been formidable in the magickal arts." I said trying to sooth his ego.

"Let's go train." And I gave him one quick hug as we got into the car and made our way down the dirt road to my home where my Uncle, Aunt, Kiedan, Croix, and apparently Gretchen Wilks awaited.

As we drove down the road, I could not help but suspect that Gavin had something to do with the theft or our Book of Shadows and just shortly after it had told me that it was also him who had stolen the Grand Grimoire. Moreover, why did Gretchen Wilks feel that I needed magickal training now more than ever?

We stopped at the driveway of my home. I put the car in park and cut off the engine. Tiegan quickly evacuated the car and stood in front of my door to open it. As I started to move, I was suddenly frozen in my seat. The skies appeared to grow dark and when I looked at Tiegan, he seemed to be frozen in time. Whispers filled my ears, dozens of voices at once not making any sense at first but then they managed to merge together to make one unified sound. The now single voice, unidentifiable as neither male nor female began to speak.

"He, the one who has come with ulterior motives has taken me from my safe haven."

"Please, great book, who has taken you?" I asked.

"He who wants to bring about the Old Ones." The book replies, still cryptic in its responses.

"Great book can you tell me the name of the one who now has you, is it Gavin McLellan?"

"Aye, it is he."

My mouth opened and my eyes grew wide with shock as things where now starting to make sense. His looks, the innuendos made, even the fight in the women's bathroom with his assistant. It all started to make sense. But that would also mean that he's behind the nightly attacks that I've been experiencing lately as well as trying to somehow subdue me through sex magick. The sky suddenly cleared and the voices disappeared leaving me frozen with shock in the driver's seat of my car. I was brought back to reality by the loud banging of Tiegan who was frantically trying to open my door and snap me out of the trance I was in. I opened the door and emerged from the vehicle still shaken by the news, my body chilled with fear. I looked at Tiegan who was now holding me.

"We need to get to the others." I finally managed to speak.

"Anora what happened, you looked as though you were in some kind of trance."

"The Book of Shadows spoke to me, and I know who took it."

Tiegan stepped back and took my hand, hastening me into the house as fast as he possibly could without ripping my arm off. He burst into the front door with me in tow, startling everyone waiting in the living room. As they all turned to look our way, Tiegan stopped and stood pulling me to stand alongside him.

"Anora knows who has stolen the Book of Shadows." He said.

I looked around at all the faces who were now focused on my next words. Taking a deep breath and blinking several times, I opened my mouth and spoke just two single words.

"Gavin McLellan."

Chapter Sixteen

"That son of a bitch." Were the first words, which broke what could have been a never-ending silence as we all stood in the living room. Croix's face showed the most disgust. Besides being an employee at the GrafX Design Company, he has had the second most familiarity with Gavin besides me. Aunt Elise and Uncle Adler both displayed the classic opened mouth expressions, a mixture of surprise and disappointment. Elder Gretchen Wilkes on the other hand, appeared unphased by the news. Her expression shown that of someone correct in his or her suspicions. I know she's lived for many years but could she have somehow foreseen this outcome and if so, why not intervene ahead of time?

I turned, as we all did, to Croix to see if he would continue talking, and of course, he was far from finished with his rant.

"Something about that obnoxious bastard rubbed me the wrong way." He continued.
"But he's just a Wiccan enthusiast, what could he want with the book?" asked Tiegan.
"He's also responsible for the theft of the Grand Grimoire." I added
"How do you know that?" Replied Aunt Elise.
"At the festival, the Book of Shadows told me in so few words, that Gavin was responsible."
"He's out to finish what he started years ago." Replied Gretchen as she took a slow sip of Jasmine tea.
"What do you mean by that Elder Gretchen?" This from Croix whose face began to show a hint of worry.
"He first took the book twenty-three years ago and used its power to open a portal to release the Old Ones." She continued.

My heart stopped beating and a wave of shock covered me like a dark cloak. I gasped and the weight of my body lightened. I closed my eyes and when I opened them again, I was looking up at familiar faces. I had fainted from shock.

Tiegan, Kiedan, and Croix looked bewildered while my Uncle, Aunt, and Elder Gretchen appeared un-phased by the revelation.

"Anora honey are you alright?" Asked Aunt Elise.

I sat up and cleared my head of the remaining fog. I wanted to ask questions but first, I had to prove I was well enough to do so. I started to stand once more feeling three sets of hands behind me offering assistance. I stood and faced my Aunt and Uncle who were standing together, my Uncle Adler holding my Aunt Elise in support.

"I need to know something, is he the hooded man who caused the disappearance of my parents when I was ten?" I asked.

Complete silence.

I waited for a moment but none of the three who seem to have some insight into what was going on had answered. I didn't have time to force the answer. If this person, this Gavin McLellan and the hooded man who took my parents were one in the same, I needed to know now.

"ANSWER ME!" I shouted.
"Yes child he is." Answered Gretchen Wilkes as she walked over to stand in front of me.
"And how long have you known this?"
"Since the imitation festival when he placed his hand on the Great Book." She replied.

The thought that entered my mind must have shown on my face. I remembered hearing the Book of Shadows speak to me, warning me about Gavin's intentions the night of the festival. I thought back when I first met him at the office when we took on a project for him and the encounter I had in the women's bathroom with his assistant. I couldn't help but feel dirty wondering if he was also somehow responsible for the attacks on me with the use of sex magick. My stomach turned and my throat contracted as if I were about to vomit the very thoughts which had entered my mind.

"Anora are you alright you look ill?" Asked Uncle Adler who until now has not said a word however, I could tell that he was worried.

"It all makes sense now doesn't it Elder Gretchen?" I said, implying that I had reached the same conclusion which she had done some time ago.

I turned towards where she stood, her face frozen with the look of concern and a tad bit of guilt. All this time she knew that this would occur. It was unfinished business on Gavin's part but why did she leave the rest of us in the dark about it? Now that it's come to past, we are all in danger. Everyone in the room had now turned their attention towards Gretchen Wilkes. She showed no signs of intimidation towards the individuals who were now waiting on her next words. Gretchen blinked twice and took in a deep breath as if what she was about to say would require it.

"Yes I knew this would happen sooner or later but I did not know which form the beast would use to carry out its agenda." She began.

"Beast?" We all seem to say simultaneously.

"Aye, what you have come to know as Gavin McLellan, is in fact, is more creature than man. He's been corrupted by dark magick for so long that it has eaten away at every shred of his once human self. But in return, he's been given eternal life. However, he must take on human forms for his true self is just too hideous to look upon. It is for that reason that when not in human form, the creature travels the lands shrouded in a cloak of pure darkness." Said Gretchen as she then took another sip of her tea.

"Cloak as in a black hooded cloak?" I asked.

"Aye." She responded.

My jaw dropped as did the cup in my hands which I could no longer feel. "Him." I thought to myself. "It's him, the figure that took my parents when I was ten." This creature has come back to finish what he was denied long ago, to release The Old Ones and in return, gain power.

"So he wants to release the Old Ones from their prison?" I asked.

"Aye that is correct, but we couldn't be sure it was him until now when he revealed himself." Replied Gretchen.

"But how did you know?" I asked.

"I heard the book when it revealed it to you that night."

"So we know that son of a bitch has both the Grand Grimoire and our Book of Shadows and we know what he plans to do with them, so why aren't we preparing ourselves?" Said Croix in a frustrated and angered voice.

I closed my eyes and pictured that faithful afternoon when my parents were taken away from me. I remembered the brave tree that held me while they fought the black hooded figure now known as Gavin McLellan. I thought of how Gretchen knew that one day this creature dressed in human skin would return to reclaim the books and try once more to fulfill his dark desires. The thought of the nights when I felt someone or something trying to bewitch me with sex magick, recalling how Gavin looked and talked to me especially at the festival. These thoughts manifested into a mass of swirling bile deep in my stomach and just like that, it shot up to the surface of my mouth and I flung my upper body forward and released it onto the hardwood floor.

"Lady and Lord, Anora are you alright?" Said Aunt Elise as she quickly rushed over to where I was now hunched over.

My eyes were closed but I could feel hands on my arms waist and hair. Before I even opened them again, I could sense that the hands belonged to Aunt Elise, Uncle Adler, and Croix. My body became warm until it caused my eyes to burn and tear. I was now relieved from the sickening reality of the past events and now, I wanted some alone time. I stood upright, flinging my head back and taking in a deep breath. Once I've tasted the clean air, I exhaled and stood looking at everyone who now seemed more concerned with me than the topic of conversation. But I still wanted to be by myself if nothing more than to get myself together.

"I'm going to my room to recuperate." I said.

Before anyone could respond, I walked over and proceeded up the stairs. I reached the threshold of my room and stood for a second to listen for any sounds or movement from below, nothing. They obviously agreed with me that I needed time to myself, or at least, they weren't going to stop me. So I walked into the room and closed the door behind me.

As I walked over towards my altar I could feel a tingle in the air, a tingle which seemed to resonate throughout my body causing me to stop for a moment and take notice. But the distraction didn't sway me from my purpose for being in the room. I needed time, guidance and most of all help. I continued to walk until I was standing in front of the altar looking at the two statues of the Goddess and God. I closed my eyes and with my mind's voice, I begged them for help.

"Lady and Lord please help me to deal with whatever is yet to come." I began. "Please send aid to me to help protect all and to return that which belongs to us from the hands of the one who seeks to use it for evil intent."

I concentrated on my parents, envisioning their figures in my mind. When I could see them as clear as day, I asked them to help me. I focused hard on the statues of the Goddess and God atop my alter until my entire body grew warm from the magick. I closed my eyes once more and with my mind's voice I called out to the Lady and Lord for a sign. I opened my eyes once more and looked around the room. Two orbs the size of soccer balls appeared out of thin air and flew around the room. The orbs felt warm when the past me and glowed of bluish-white light which made me feel calm and at ease while I watched them dance from corner to corner finally coming to rest on the floor in front of me.

The orbs began to take shape until I was face to face with a ladybug the size of a one-year-old bear cub and a hamster that was a big as an eagle. The two looked at me then what appeared to be smiles formed on their faces.

"Hello Anora." The two said in unison.
"Hello there, and who might you two be?" I replied.

"I'm Iliana and this is Kriani." Said the large hamster as she pointed to the large ladybug.

"How did you come to be here?" I asked.

"We heard your summons so we came." Said Kriani who began to beat her large wings for no apparent reason.

I paused for a moment attempting to ascertain how these two came to the conclusion that I had summoned them. I remembered saying a prayer and, like a psychic slap on the face it hit me. Aunt Elise once told me during one of our spell casting sessions, "A prayer is like a spell so just as you're to be careful with what you wish for, so to must you take caution with what you say while praying." I guess someone heard me when I asked for help and sent me these two interesting entities.

Gretchen Wilks came out of the house moving more cautiously slower than her normal pace, she was staring upwards and towards the open field behind the center square of the community. If I'd not known better, I'd swear the look on her face was one of horror. Just then there was a loud boom as if someone had dropped an atom bomb right in the center of the community. The sky grew increasingly dark and the air smelled of brimstone. Uncle Adler and Aunt Elise emerged from the house to stand behind Gretchen. Kiedan, Tiegan, and Croix ran from the house and stood on the front lawn. I glanced at my two new companions whose eyes were now glowing yellow, the look of anger shown on their faces such as how dogs look when they sense an enemy.

"Iliana, Kriani what's wrong?" I asked.

The two turned to look at me, their eyes still aglow.

"It's him." they said in unison.

Thick black clouds swirled overhead. In the distance, atop the roof of the temple stood a cloaked figure, its arms outstretched. I looked over at the house to where the others were standing.

"Come forth my brethren and pave the way for The Old Ones."
The cloaked figure yelled.

Balls of fire began raining down from the swirling blackness in
the sky. Each one that hit the ground transformed into a black scaly
lizard-like demon with red eyes. I looked once more at my Aunt,
Uncle, and the others with horror.

"Let's go Knights." Yelled Croix as he clapped his hands
together then parting them which produced a glowing white sword.
Kiedan and Tiegan took two steps forward and with an eye blink, they
shifted into two large beasts, covered in jet black fur, with black claws,
razor sharped teeth, glowing white eyes and thick scaly tails.

The three ran towards the horde of demons. I saw in the distance
a bright bluish-white dome covering the meeting hall. The Elders had
cast a protection spell to keep the people of our community safe while
the Celtic Knights and those like my Aunt, Uncle, and Gretchen Wilks
defended our community.

"Bring me the one called Anora." Bellowed the cloaked figure
and in that moment, I realized who it was.

I noticed that the voice, although slightly huskier than normal,
belonged to Gavin McLellan. I saw The Great Book and the Grand
Grimoire hovering over his head. Somehow he's managed to use the
books to open a doorway in the sky for Goddess knows what to come
through. Everything around me suddenly went silent as my brain had
its epiphany for the year. It was happening again, but this time, my
parents weren't here but inside, I was that ten-year-old frightened girl.

I was so preoccupied with my momentary mind trip back in
time, that I hadn't noticed the four demons which suddenly encircled
me. By the time I regained my composure, it was too late to cast a
protection spell. Just then, I heard the voices of my two new
companions who I had forgotten were still next to me.

"We've got this Anora." They said in unison with glowing
yellow eyes and what appeared to be grins on their faces.

I couldn't believe what I just heard. Here are, although larger than their average species, this hamster, and ladybug ready to take on four scaly demons. My initial thought was that the poor things although big, would still be torn to pieces. Boy did I learn fast how not to judge a book by its cover. The demons inched towards us savoring the moment when Iliana with an eye blink grew to about ten feet tall, with razor sharp fangs and claws. Her soft fur was now a rough bristle. Kriani also grew to ten feet, her ladybug wings retracted and her body became a hardened pitch-black shell with blood red streaks. She too was armed with razor sharped fangs and claws. I always tend to ask for the Lady and Lord to help me and it looks as if they answered my prayers with these two. These once sweet looking creatures were now ripping apart the four demons as if they were made of tissue paper.

My jaw would have dropped if not for the adrenaline rush of the moment taking over. I hadn't realized that I was now alone. Aunt Elise, Uncle Adler, and Elder Gretchen had gone to help protect the community while Iliana and Kriani had gone off to level the playing field by taking out more of Gavin's scaly demons. I felt the air grow increasingly still, the sky above me was now a dark gray with swirling black clouds. I heard my name being whispered on the wind but it seemed to come from every direction I turned. I looked behind me once more in the direction of the whisper to suddenly stand face to hooded face with Gavin.

Before I could react to his presence, he flung his right hand upwards and without warning, my body flew backward sending me into a group of wooden barrels, the force of the impact turned several of them into piles of wood. When I opened my eyes and was able to focus, there standing over me was Gavin black hood and all. He looked around at the various battles between his demons and the Celtic Knights, along with my Aunt, Uncle, Gretchen Wilks and my two new companions, then slowly turning his gaze back to me with a smirk and a cocked head he whispered.

"Alone at least."

I started to stand, fixing my gaze towards Gavin who stood there savoring the moment, the Grand Grimoire and the Book of Shadows hovering on each side of him and a smirk on his face.

"Oh how I'd love to wipe that smirk off of his face." I thought to myself. I took a quick glance at the Book of Shadows and notice that there was an eye in the middle of the Triquetra and it was crying. Whatever Gavin was making it do, it clearly did not want to do it and was sorrowful for having been forced to.

I could feel its pain as if hundreds of souls were all crying at once. Gavin let me stand and there we were face to face like a magickal Mexican standoff. He drew back the hood appearing confident and sure of himself. He clutched the two books underneath his arm and put his free hand on his hip, smirking at me the entire time.

"My dear Anora, it would seem that after all these years we've come full circle."
"You, it was you that day. You took my parents from me you bastard." I said with as much hatred in my voice as I could project.
"They wouldn't have had to sacrifice themselves if they hadn't kept me from my objective."
"You're a bastard." I hissed.
"Call me what you will, but I will finish what I started long ago and you will help to ensure my success."

I wanted to strike him across the face as hard as I could, but before I could even lift my hand to do so, he raised the books over his head and I become completely paralyzed where I stood. No matter how hard I tired, none of my limbs would respond. "How did he do that without uttering a single word?" I thought. I could still move my eyes so I looked as far as my peripheral vision would allow. Everyone else seemed to have not been affected by whatever what holding me in place.

I tried once more to move but it felt as though my body was one large frozen mass. I had to get free but how? I could still use my mind and then it came to me, "I could call for help telepathically."

I took a deep breath as Gavin was now standing in breathing distance from me, the books at his side and his free hand now resting on my left shoulder. His face adorned a triumphant smirk. I gave my face a frightened look so as to keep Gavin in his state of confidence. I closed my eyes, but before I could even think the word help, a voice spoke to me.

"Worry not child for we are here with you." Spoke a soft feminine voice. Just the sound alone filled me with a sense of calm. Just then, I could feel my limbs once more and without hesitation, I jumped back, outstretched my arms with my palms opened while still facing Gavin.

"GET AWAY FROM ME YOU SON OF A BITCH!" I yelled.

My palms grew warm and once the word bitch had exited from my lips, the heat from my palms shot forward hitting Gavin and propelling him several feet backward onto the ground. I stood there and looked first at my hands which were still warm for the blast of energy that came from them, then I turned my attention to where Gavin had landed. He started to sit up slowly. I watched him stagger to his feet clearly disoriented. He wiped the line of blood from the side of his mouth and gave a painful laugh.

"Well now, I can't say I saw that coming." He said.
"Stop this madness Gavin, it's not too late." I pleaded.

Suddenly I noticed that the books were no longer in his hand and at that moment, I think he shared the same thought as we both glanced over to where they now lay.

Chapter Seventeen

Both of our eyes were fixed on the books which laid on a bed of white lilies. The heat in my palms finally dissipated. In the distance, I could hear the sounds of the continued clash between the Celtic Knights, my Aunt, Uncle, Gretchen Wilks and the other Elders, Iliana, Kriani, and Gavin's demons. I wanted to turn to see where my new companions were and if they were alright but then again after seeing their transformations, I'm sure they were fine. Gavin held out his right hand in a grabbing gesture. He drew his arm back then making several thrusts out and back as if he were expecting the books to come to him but they remained motionless.

"Come to me you damnit." He hissed, but the books did not budge.
"I command you." He yelled but still they remained steadfast to where they lay.

His eyes now took on a yellow glow. I could see the frustration and anger on his face. Taking another look, at the books, I again heard a voice echo to me inside my head.

"You have it within you to defeat he who stands before you." The voice said but this time, it was masculine and as it spoke, I felt a wash of energy wash over me, giving me the feeling of safety. I closed my eyes once more and uttered the four words which would forever change my life.

"Take me O Great Books."

My body flared with heat, every part of me tingled with energy. I looked around to see that the battle had stopped and everyone on both sides stood in gaping awe at whatever they saw in me. I felt lighter than normal as if my body had become like a feather. Then I noticed that even Gavin himself now displayed that jaw-dropping look.

I was floating, at least four feet off the ground, my entire body shimmering with a blue-white light, and my eyes were ablaze with white light. Lady and Lord you helped me after all. My mind was filled with spells, chants, and all sorts of incantations. It was as if the books themselves now dwelled inside me. Once more both the male and female voices spoke.

"You have been chosen to dispel this evil." They said in unison.

Gavin stepped back, his expression turned back to that evil arrogance.

"You excitingly interesting little bitch."
"I know now, it was you that caused my parents disappearance." I said.
"Indeed, they were all that stood between me and the liberation of the Old Ones."
"And I guess it would stand to reason that despite their demise, they succeeded in stopping you."
"True my dear, but you were to be my ticket to success this time around." He snickered.
"Not today or any day asshole." I replied.

With the current situation at hand and thoughts of my parents, I had forgotten that I was still floating and burning with energy but now, I was filled with anger. I took another look around and with every one of Gavin's minions that I saw, my anger flared in crackles of energy.

I wanted them gone, to no longer harm those I cared about. There was something else that I had forgotten which arrived about five minutes ago. It was passed midnight and my birthday had arrived. I completely forgot with all that has happened lately. Stupid me, I took my concentration away from Gavin. When I focused my attention back to him, he flung his left hand into the air and yelled.

"YOU ARE MINE ANORA."

A violent wave of energy smacked into me, throwing me backward again, this time, causing me to slam against a large tree.

I was no longer floating however, I was still somehow aglow with that bluish-white light. I could see Gavin picking up the books and as I quickly looked to both the left and right of me, I saw the various battles erupt once more. This had to stop, I wanted it to stop, but most of all, I wanted Gavin McLellan to die.

Gavin stood tall and confident once more, with the books again in his possession. He held them upwards and in a voice, which I could best describe as half man, half monster, he called forth the Old Ones.

"ANCIENT RULERS OF THE LAND, YOUR SERVANT SUMMONS YOU FOURTH TO CLAIM YOUR RIGHTFUL PLACE IN THIS REALM." He commanded.

The sky filled with thick dark gray storm clouds, lightning ran back and forth, and suddenly there was a swirling black hole in the center of it all. Everyone stopped fighting and Gavin's minions looked on with joy while the rest of us looked on in horror. It was happening again. I was that ten-year-old girl witnessing this terrible thing occurring but this time, I thought to myself, my parents weren't here to stop it. Suddenly, like a streak of mental energy, the thought came to me. If the books could communicate to me, perhaps I can communicate with them. Lady and Lord help me once more please.

"Here goes nothing." I thought to myself. I stood up against the tree, stretched out my arms as if to welcome an embrace, and yelled.
"ANCIENT BOOKS OF WISDOM COME AND BE WITH ME NOW."

The books flew from Gavin's hands and as I watched it fly towards me I thought of my mother, father, Aunt Elise, Uncle Adler, and everyone whom I cared for and who right now, were looking for me to finish this. It was my birthday and apparently I have been given the power to do so. I watched as the books came to me, the expression on Gavin's face was part evil grin and part discuss. The books pressed against my chest but they didn't stop moving forward. I could feel their rectangular shape but as they continued to press onward, their mass slowly dissipated.

It wasn't until I looked downward that I saw that they were pushing themselves into my body however, I did not feel any pain.

I, as I'm sure everyone else in view was, watched as the books slowly disappeared into my chest until they were gone altogether. My body flared up with energy once more. I closed my eyes and saw pages of spells, incantations, chants and all other writings that were once housed within the books.

"NO!" Gavin shouted. His eyes shining with that yellowish glow, his teeth clenched tight.

I still housed the anger and desire to end this. Swinging my arm from left to right and chanted.

"Those who have harmed others, I send you into that which swirls above."

One by one, Gavin's minions turned to ashes and rose upwards towards the swirling blackness above. Gavin's face bore the look of one who just has experienced sheer terror. The yellow glow in his eyes now and he stood still surrounded by those who would want him dead. Gavin face now bore that handsome appearance that I was first introduced to when we met at the Graphics Design agency. He looked innocent almost sad.

"Please Anora, I ask that you grant me mercy." He said in a soft calm voice.
"You tried to kill us all by bringing those monsters back to this realm and you want me to grant you mercy?"

I raised my right hand slowly and Gavin's body began to rise upward towards the swirling black hole. There was a loud roar that echoed like thunder, causing us all to turn our gaze up towards the blackness. Four giant tentacles descended downward to where Gavin was still ascending.

"Anora please I beg you to have mercy." He screamed as the tentacles were now mere inches above him.

"My parents are gone because of you, it's time you paid for what you've done."

"Please someone make her stop." He cried.

No one moved to intervene on his behalf. The tentacles now reached him and slowly wrapped themselves around his neck and waist. There were tiny mouths with razor sharp teeth at the end of each of them. The mouths started feeding on his flesh as he began screaming and pleading. We all stood and watched as they carried him upwards screaming into the black hole.

As he disappeared from sight, the black hole quickly started to close. We heard him shriek what would be his last words.

"ANORA!"

With that, the black hole closed completely. The thick dark gray clouds quickly dissipated bringing forth a cloudless starry night with a wonderfully bright waning moon. The air was warm and refreshing with the smell of fresh lilies. I closed my eyes and took in a deep breath. As I let it out, the glow which surrounded me started to fade until it was completely gone from view. My eyes were back to their original state and I finally was aware of the fact that I was now back on solid ground.

Chapter Eighteen

I raised my head to the sky and took another deep breath. "It's over." I said in a soft whisper as I watched the twinkling stars dance around in the sky. I thought of my parents and how much I wish they were here with me now. I ignored the goings on around me and remained focused on the activity in the sky. Amongst all the stars which displayed their radiance, there were two that appeared to be getting brighter and pulsated like that of a human heart beating. I was transfixed on these two stars as the started to increase in their radiance while slowly descending coming to hover just feet from where I stood.

The stars turned into two bright orbs as they touched the ground. Their small size suddenly changing as they grew just as the orbs which spawned my two new guardians did during our initial meeting. The now life-sized orbs began taking shapes, both beginning to give the outline of human bodies. Their glow felt warm and comforting as if I were familiar with them and them with me. I felt compassion, love and protection as their shapes became more defined, one male the other female. The male stood at six feet five inches tall with broad shoulders, a thick muscular build, with short auburn hair. Moreover, there appear to be streaks of sunlight running through it. He had no visible facial hair except for thin eyebrows which like his hair were the also auburn. The female counterpart stood at five feet four inches tall with dark brown hair that fell down to her backside.

As with her male counterpart, she also bore streaks in her hair, however, hers were of blue-white light almost resembling moonlight. Her body was slender except for her perfectly busty breasts. Her face was soft with thin dark brown eyebrows, high cheek bones, a thin nose and thin red lips. They were both wearing royal blue hooded robes but their hoods were down to show their full face and hair. They stepped closer until we were directly in front of each other and it wasn't until they were practically in kissing distance that I realized exactly who I was looking at.

"Mother Father is it really you?" I said after letting out an opened mouth gasp.

They stood there smiling with sparkling white teeth. I couldn't help but to smile back. Taking a quick look around I saw that everyone in the community had gathered around us including my new guardian friends Iliana and Kriani who have now resumed their original forms. I turned back towards my parents and the three of us shared a long embrace. Tears ran down my cheeks despite my best efforts to hold both of them back. They felt warm and soft and I couldn't' help but try to squeeze them tighter thinking that if I held them tightly enough, they couldn't be taken away from me again. I drew back from the embrace and gave them each a kiss on their cheeks, whispering in their ear that I loved them. The three of us stood there until my mother finally broke our joyful silence.

"Happy Birthday sweetie, we missed you so much."
"Yes dear, Happy Birthday, we are so very proud of you." This coming from my father.
"Mother Father, I thought I would never see you again after that day."
"We were always there with you child, watching you grow and waiting for just this moment when we would be together once more." Explained my Mother.
"What happened to you that day?" I asked.
"We had to close the portal before the Old Ones could enter through but because it had been opened by the Grand Grimoire, the only way to close it was for the two of us to combine our energies into one spell. However, in casting such a spell it took our physical forms and once the portal was closed, and the Grand Grimoire transported to a safe place, we had just enough of our essence to place ourselves somewhere that we could regain our strength in time undisturbed." Explained my Father.
"If you were watching me all this time why didn't you contact me?" I asked.
"Oh but we did, we answered you every time you called to us." Said my Mother.
"I don't understand."
"You don't remember calling to us all this time?"

"No."

"Then allow us to refresh your memory." Said my Father.

"Lady and Lord help me." They both said in unison. My mouth opened with a gasp and my eyes grew wide with disbelief. I couldn't believe what I was hearing until Elder Gretchen, who unbenounced to me had walked over to stand to my left, had placed her right hand on my shoulder to get my attention. I turned my head to her in acknowledgment.

"My dear Anora, I guess now you understand what your Aunt meant when she said that you were special." She said softly. She then turned to look at the individuals in front of me and gave them a humble bow, acknowledging their presence by respectfully saying "Mother Goddess, Father God, merry meet to you."

They both gave her an equally respectable smiling bow then looked back to me.

"Anora we will always be with you and we hope that you enjoy the two companions we sent to you." My Mother said with a smile.

"Why do I detect a but coming?" I replied.

"Yes you are correct, although you are our daughter we cannot remain in this form for too long. This is why we entrusted you to your Aunt and Uncle all these years." Said Father.

"I'm losing you once more aren't I?"

"You are never going to lose us dear, we are the Goddess and God and you are the product of the love we have for one another." Said Mother.

I wanted to be sad but for some reason their words made sense to me and I did not shed a tear but instead I smiled at them both, then leaned in to hug them once more before standing back with a smile.

"This is the best birthday present I could ever have hoped to receive." I said still smiling.

"We'd like to, at least spend it with you until we must return to the heavens at sunrise." Said Father.

"I'd like that very much."

"Please grace our community with your presence." Said Elder Gretchen.

They both nodded in acceptance and we all walked to the temple for a celebration long overdue. Iliana and Kriani came to walk alongside us. The entire community accompanied us into the temple. We gathered as much of the festival's feast that wasn't destroyed in the fight and laid it out on tables inside the temple. Music began to play from out of nowhere, my mother waved her hand over a bucket of well water and in an instant, it turned into sweet tasting red wine.

The Book of Shadows as well as the Grand Grimoire were now a part of me. Therefore, the Elders removed the stand where it once laid and replaced it with a small alter adorning it with fresh flowers, white candles and a gold goblet carved with the image of a triple moon. Once the last person had entered the temple to partake in the celebration, the large metal doors closed on their own and there was a calm silence outside.

Undenounced to everyone inside, there was one individual who choose not to partake in the festivities. A lone thin figure covered in a dark grey hooded cloak came to stand in front of the temple. The figure held out its right arm to reveal its thin shape and the presence of fingernails, deducing that in fact the figure was a woman. She opened her hand and in an instant, a silver athame appeared. The large knife had a carving of a snake holding a bone in its mouth. She pointed the knife at the temple doors and removed her hood with her free hand. Silvia Blakely, Gavin's assistant, gave an evil grin as she raised the athame to the sky.

"So mote it be Anora Rhianlugh, so mote it be." She whispered. Then with a slow turn, she disappeared.